Miracles
and
Murders

Miracles and Murders

A Collection of Short but Epic Stories

by

S. A. Philp

Paperback ISBN: 978-1-80227-577-3
eBook ISBN: 978-1-80227-578-0

*Thanks to the Publishing Push team,
Sussex Business Bureau and
Pauline Philp.*

*This book is dedicated to
my future grandchildren.*

*Never look up to anyone
who thinks they're superior.*

*Never look down on anyone
who thinks they're inferior.*

Introduction

Imagine dreaming of a colour never seen before
Or discovering a new horizon like a conquistador.
Will you find death or will you find glory
As you turn each page in the power of a story?

Contents

Stories

To Valhalla and Back

INTRODUCTION

MY NAME IS MAGNUS GUNNERSON.
I AM A SEVENTH SON OF A
SEVENTH SON.
I COME FROM A LONG BLOODLINE OF
GREAT KINGS AND VIKING WARRIORS.
THIS IS MY STORY OF A QUEST INTO
THE UNKNOWN
AND A VOYAGE OF DISCOVERY.
A TALE OF ADVENTURE, DEATH
AND GLORY.

Legend has it my father, Gunner, killed all of his elder brothers to become king. Whether this is true, I do not know or care.
I just know I love all my six elder brothers, so I will never become king.

What I do know is that I will leave my mark on this mortal world for my destiny is to become

A VIKING LEGEND.

THE END IS UPON ME

Two days ago I was found barely alive, washed up on a beach on the north coast of Spain. I was taken to a small monastery nearby where I have been well fed, watered and nursed. I know this because the head of this monastery is Father Benitez.

Father Benitez is a well-educated man and speaks many languages, including my Nordic tongue. It is good that Benitez speaks my language for I have a story to tell, a story I have instructed Benitez to write down so all the world will know. But he must write quickly for I have not long to live. My wounds are deep and I have lost much blood, and when I close my eyes, I see the great halls of Valhalla.

For this part is the end of my story. The beginning starts five seasons and many moons ago.

THE BEGINNING

Five seasons and many moons ago on the West Coast of Ireland, in the year 1,000 A.D.

We raid, we kill, we pillage, we plunder, we rape, we burn, we kill and we kill again. Are we good, are we bad? Are we right, are we wrong? I do not know. I just know we are Vikings and this is what we do. For this is our way.

Tonight we camp on the beach. We build a bonfire and celebrate for the raids are over and soon we will be sailing home.

Tonight is a special night for me, for my life is about to change forever. As the early hours come and pass and bodies sleep where they fall, I look into the dying embers of the bonfire and see my destiny. For a seventh son of a seventh son has the power to see the future but only when the future wants to be seen.

I have seen visions before. I predicted the death of my mother and foresaw our raids on Ireland. In this dream-like vision, I see a new horizon and a whole new world. As the sun rises, so do my hopes, plans, dreams and aspirations.

After a late, hungover breakfast, I gathered the tribe for my announcement.

"My dear father, King Gunner, my beloved brothers and my fellow warriors. I will not be returning home with you. For last night, in the dying embers, I foresaw my destiny. Last year the great Leif Erickson, the son of Eric the Red, discovered a new land not far from Greenland. He named it Vineland. I believe Vineland to be just the northern tip of a whole new world. I, Magnus Gunnerson, intend to sail west straight across the great ocean. I know not how far or how long this will take, but I know there is a great land across the water. I cannot achieve this on my own, so I ask whether there are any among you, who will join my voyage of discovery and become legends in the history of mortal man."

THE CREW

Some of the tribe stepped forward, and one by one they pledged their allegiance to me.

"I, Helvin, will go with you. We have been best friends all of our lives and you know I will never leave your side. I will follow you to the edge of the world, or even into hell."

"I am Toki, and this is my twin brother Tovi. We will join your quest and find glory for the tribe."

"My name is Rolf. I am only young but I yearn for adventure."

"I am Torstein, father of Rolf. He is all I have, so I will sail the same seas."

"I am Olaf. You will need a navigator, and no one knows the stars better than I."

I embraced them all, then my father, the king, spoke.

"Magnus, my youngest son. I will miss you but I know you will do me proud. May the great god Odin watch over you and your men, and may the mighty god Thor protect you all. Brave Vikings, your king and tribe salute you."

With that, the whole tribe hollered out, bashed their shields and stomped their feet. It was a truly warm-felt, emotional, thunderous salute and farewell.

We were now seven strong.

I, Magnus, was the fastest sword arm of our tribe. Then there was Helvin, my lifelong friend, a giant of a man who could wield a double-headed axe like a tornado; Toki and Tovi, the red-headed twins, both great archers and oarsmen; young Rolf, with not much experience but eager and brave; his father Torstein, sixty-plus years but still with plenty of fight inside him; Olaf, a hairy beast of a man who wore a patch as he had lost an eye in battle, but with his one good eye, he would see our path across the water.

We needed three more for the journey. I picked out two of our Irish captives. I gave them freedom for the promise of their loyalty. They were Aidan and Flynn, two fierce Irish warriors.

The last of my crew was Dagna. We had captured Dagna but only after he had killed many of our tribe, most of them with his bare hands. He was an animal, so we had caged him like one. He had tattooed skin, red eyes and long, white hair, a true freak of nature. He could not speak, only howl as he had no tongue. It had been cut from his mouth when he was a child. My father had planned to take him home and sacrifice him to the gods. The rest of the crew thought I was mad to take him with us, but when I looked into those red eyes, I could see a man ready to trust and follow me. We would keep Dagna chained up at all times.

Now we were ten.

GODSPEED

Over the next two weeks, we built a small longship called a Knarr. We built it for strength and speed. It was twenty-five feet long and ten feet across in the middle, narrowing at both ends. It had a large, single sail and a steering oar at the stern. It had eight rowing oars and a covered hull at the front for supplies. At the front we stored water, dried meat, salted fish, oatcakes and weapons.

We named our boat Godspeed in honour of the gods.

It was the start of spring when we began our quest. Olaf and I would take turns to steer and navigate. We chained Dagna at the rear where he could row with two oars. The rest of the crew would rotate, either manning the sail or taking a single oar. If the weather was bad, we could lower the sail and use it as a shelter.

We had nine good days before we hit trouble. During those nine days, my crew realised the wisdom of bringing Dagna along with us, for he was like a creature possessed. He would only stop rowing for food, water, a shit and a few hours' sleep. His red eyes burned from a fire deep down inside.

On the tenth day into our voyage, we hit troubled waters. It was mid-spring and mid-afternoon; the sun was skin-burning hot, with barely a breeze.

Suddenly Olaf roared, "Sea monster! A sea monster! It's heading straight for us – row faster, you bastards, faster!"

It was a whale twice the size of our boat. It dived and resurfaced, each time getting closer, no matter how fast we rowed. Finally it caught up with us and brushed passed us, spinning the boat full circle. Aidan fell overboard. Flynn dived into the sea to save him. Then the monster flapped its huge tail, creating an almighty splash and a wave that engulfed the boat.

"Bail out before we sink and drown!" I shouted. "We will not fill our bellies with seawater. We will not die on this day, and Godspeed will not sink to an ocean grave."

We bailed out the boat with all our hearts, a couple of buckets, our helmets and clasped hands. We did not stop until the hull was dry.

There was a cry from the starboard side. "Help! Over here – pull us in! We're not fish and our clothes are getting a bit damp." It was Flynn spluttering but smiling.

He had hold of Aidan, who was alive and well.

The sea monster had gone, and we were all alive and in good spirits. So onwards we sailed.

TWENTY-SEVEN DAYS

The weather changed. The next six days became rough and stormy. With strong winds and strong arms, we made good progress but without any sight of land. The weather calmed down again, which was good for young Rolf. Rolf had no legs for the sea and had been sick on every rough day. His father, Torstein, was a great fisherman so we ate plenty of fresh fish. This was now our only food source; after twenty days at sea, our supplies had run out. We still had fresh water, but this would now be rationed.

We were on a journey no man had ventured before, so we had little idea of how many days this quest would take. But I had no doubt in my head that we would find land across the other side of this ocean.

I believed and the crew believed in me.

Seven days later.

"Land yonder! Land yonder! Over there, look, cast your eyes and see," hollered Olaf.

"He's right!" said Helvin. "There is land! We've made it. We put our trust in Magnus and he has delivered."

After twenty-seven days at sea, we had finally spotted land. We all cheered and opened a barrel of ale that we had saved for that moment.

We all drank, shook hands and hugged one another. I turned and looked to the rear of the boat. There was Dagna, still rowing.

"Set him free," I ordered.

"Are you sure about this?" replied Helvin.

I nodded my head. I was sure.

Helvin swung his axe and sliced through the chains. Time froze and we all stood like statues until Dagna stood up and stretched. He looked to the skies and then howled like a wolf. He stared at us all with his fire-red eyes. Then he smiled and we all relaxed. We all shook his hand and drank ale with him. Dagna had a certain look upon his face, the look of a man who had never known trust or friendship before.

He was now one of us.

After twenty-seven days, we had become ten friends. The first ten to cross the great ocean, and we would be the first ten to step foot on the soil of a new world.

A NEW WORLD

We landed on a beautiful, sandy beach and pulled Godspeed ashore. The twins and I went inland to hunt for food. The rest of the crew stayed and built a shelter to hide and protect the boat. It was a stunning land with tall trees and freshwater streams. It was a land with green grass and blue mountains. We soon found deer. Toki and Tovi both shot their arrows straight into the neck of a magnificent stag. We gutted the stag and returned to the others. Toki and Tovi argued the whole way back about whose arrow had struck first. I could not tell the twins apart, let alone their arrows.

The whole time, I had a strange sense of being watched. I felt eyes upon us from all directions. I wondered if us ten were alone or were people here already? Maybe hundreds, maybe thousands, and how vast was this new world? I had more questions than answers, but for now, it was just good to eat fresh meat again and have a full belly.

Over the next month, we built a fort, fished the waters and hunted the land.

It was a bountiful new world, but we all sensed that we were not alone in it.

THE FIRST MEETING

It was now the month of June by our reckoning, and the sun was high and hot when we first saw them.

Torstein and his son Rolf were working on the fort while the rest of us were out hunting.

They came at us from out of the trees. They were strange-looking savages with sunburnt skin and dark, pony-tailed hair adorned with feathers.

They threw flimsy spears at us and shot arrows from small, weak bows which barely scratched our shields. We retaliated quickly. The twins fired their superior bows and arrows, killing at least half a dozen in two blinks of an eye. We charged at them, killing them with ease. Our shields protected us from what little they had to offer. Our swords cut, slashed and chopped at their flesh and bones, reducing them to butchered lumps of meat, dropping like shit from an arse. Helvin went through them like a whirlwind, his large axe taking heads clean off, while Dagna went about his business, kicking, punching, butting, gouging and even biting.

The eight of us had slaughtered over thirty of them without loss, just cuts and bruises. The rest of the red-skinned savages ran like chickens from a fox. They were clearly no match for Vikings and warriors.

THE WISE ONE

We didn't see them again until two weeks later. About twenty redskins turned up outside our fort; they came in peace this time, bearing gifts.

They brought us animal skins, fruit and necklaces. There were also women among them this time. We let them enter the fort but stayed alert and ready for any trouble.

Their wise man came forward.

He called himself Chia Chau, which meant Red Scar. After much sign language and drawings in the dirt, we had a rough understanding of each other. His tribe were the Tuscarora and stood silent and proud next to him, was their chief, Black Feathers. They sought peace and for us to protect them against their enemy. At the end of each summer, an enemy tribe called the Shawnee would cross the north-westerly river and raid their camps.

I agreed to peace and protection for them, for I liked the idea of starting a new kingdom in this new world, but there could be only one ruler, one king and one chief.

I raised up a single finger and declared, "One chief."

Red Scar retorted, "One chief, Black Feathers chief."

I argued back, "No! One chief, Magnus. Magnus chief." And so it went on.

As fast as a strike of lightning, my sword was unleashed and plunged into the heart of Black Feathers. He dropped to his knees, his eyes closed and his face bit the dirt before my feet.

Wailing, panic and anger engulfed the Tuscarora tribe, but Red Scar calmed them down, and before long he had them bowing and chanting, "Magnus chief, Magnus chief."

Red Scar was truly a very wise man indeed.

A NEW BEGINNING

After two days of mourning Black Feathers, the Tuscarora returned to our fort. This time, the whole tribe came, bringing all they possessed with them. There were more than two hundred of them – men, women and children heading our way.

Helvin smiled as he spoke to me. "You know what, Magnus? We're gonna need a bigger fort."

I laughed but I knew he was right. We had many a long day ahead of us all.

Over July and August, we worked alongside the Tuscarora. We surrounded the fort with a wooden perimeter wall, and the redskins set up their camps within the safety of these walls. We hunted, fished, skinned animals and collected firewood together. We taught them how to make better bows, arrows, spears and shields. We showed them how to salt fish, dry meat and store for the winter months ahead. Most importantly, we trained them how to fight and do battle.

The Tuscarora learnt to follow and respect us, so we did not just take or rape their women. Instead, over time, we met, fell in love and took wives to satisfy our needs.

I myself fell in love with a beautiful girl. I fell in love the moment my eyes first fell upon her. Her name was Sky Bird and she was like a bird from paradise. She had night-sky hair, red, sun-blushed skin and virgin blue eyes. We spoke few words but our love spoke plenty.

Red Scar was quick to learn our language, and he became my right-hand man. He was the link in the chain between us ten and the redskins. Red Scar was the wisest man I had ever crossed paths with, and with his help, we were beginning to build a new kingdom in a new world.

SHAWNEE ATTACK

The end of summer was upon us and we were well-prepared for the Shawnee attack. They crossed the river about seventy strong. We had lookouts near the river who fired flaming arrows high into the sky. This was our call to arms at the fort. We hid behind the perimeter walls well-armed and ready for the attack.

We waited with hushed mouths and beating hearts.

The Shawnee chased our lookouts straight towards the fort, yelling and hollering. They stopped in their tracks and just stood and stared at the wooden structures before them. They had never come across a sight like that before. Slowly they edged closer, one step at a time.

Once they were in range, I let out the battle cry.

"Oh mighty Thor, lend us your thunder so we may hammer this foe."

With that, we showed ourselves to the enemy and unleashed arrows from behind the protection of our walls.

Hundreds of arrows rained down on the Shawnee redskins and they started dropping like swatted flies. When we opened the gates, the ten of us held back as we let the Tuscarora charge out, for it was their hour of glory. They had to show the Shawnee that they were not a weak tribe and no longer easy pickings to be raided upon.

We had trained them to fight well, and they slaughtered any Shawnee that stood his ground The rest they chased back across the river.

"Take one alive!" I shouted. "The rest, no mercy!"

And no mercy was shown.

As I walked past the bloody corpses, I noticed that the Shawnee had necklaces with gold nuggets attached. When I reached the river, the Tuscarora gifted me a Shawnee prisoner.

Red Scar could speak the Shawnee language. I told Red Scar to question our captive about the gold nuggets, but our captive would not speak. I pulled out my knife. He cried out like a mountain cat as I sliced off his left ear. Then he began to talk, and he led us to a nearby cave.

Once inside the cave, we lit torches and the walls sparkled and glistened. This was a cave of gold, a cave of dreams.

We let our Shawnee prisoner free. We told him to tell his people never to cross the river again and that we would stay on our side. There would be peace between us, but if they crossed the river again, there would be a bloodbath and the river would flow red.

GOLD, WINTER AND SPRING

Summer was over. We had the autumn months ahead before the winter would hibernate us.

Red Scar and the Tuscarora made sure the fort was well-stocked to see us through the winter. Helvin, Olaf, the twins and I mined the cave, and we extracted as much gold as we could before snowfall. The Irish pair, Flynn and Aidan, would transport the nuggets back to the fort. At the fort, Dagna kept a constant fire burning, while Torstein and his son Rolf smelted the nuggets into liquid gold, then poured the liquid into moulds to form small bars of gold.

By the time the first flakes of snow had fallen, we had amassed a fortune in gold bars. The winter months were ice cold, with thick snow up to three feet deep, but we were well-accustomed to this type of weather as our homeland winters were far colder and longer. Besides, it's easy to keep warm under the cover of soft, warm bear skins with a beautiful, naked, red-skinned woman wrapped around you.

I loved Sky Bird like I had loved no other before. She was now also swollen-bellied with child. I longed for spring to come and the birth of my firstborn.

Spring came, the snow was gone and life in the new world began once more.

I shed a single tear for the first time in my life when my son was born. We named him Little Thor in honour of the God of war. Young Rolf and Flynn were also proud new fathers.

It was now a long year since we had left the coast of Ireland. A year since we had begun our quest. We had discovered a new world, built a new home and formed a well-organised tribe. We were rich with gold and life was good, but I knew this was not enough. I had to make plans for the future, which meant tough decisions had to be made.

THE PLAN

I gathered Red Scar and the ten of us and then announced my plans for the future.

"Listen up men, for I have hard words to say. You have taken me for your leader, chief and king. You have followed me, obeyed me, sacrificed and believed in me. For this, I thank you one and all. But if we are to be true legends, we must build a bigger kingdom; we must discover how vast this new world is. For this to be so, some of us will journey home with the gold. Our homeland people will then learn of what we have achieved, and then we will return here with more ships, men and women. For this is just the beginning, my friends. The future is ours to take. Torstein, you will stay and take charge while we are gone. Rolf, you will also stay and help your father. Aidan and Flynn, I once promised you your freedom and I will not take that away, so you will both stay.

"I will sail home with Helvin, Olaf, Dagna and the twins. Red Scar and three of his strongest men will travel with us. I know it will be hard to leave your wives, but I will also be leaving mine and my son. We will miss our good lives here, but we will return. History will remember the ten of us that set out on a voyage into the unknown, for we will be legends. These are my words, and now I ask, do you still believe in me?"

One by one, the men began to chant my name,
then all together in chorus.

"Magnus! Magnus! Magnus!"

I shed a single tear for only the second time in my life.

THE RAGING FIRE

We spent the next week restoring Godspeed to sail once again. We stocked the boat with plenty of food, water and, of course, the gold.

Sky Bird cried herself to sleep every night on hearing my plans. It would break my heart to leave my wife and my son, little Thor, behind, but what must be done, must be done.

One hot, sticky night, I saw a vision of a great fire raging. I kept this vision to myself for I was not sure of its meaning, but I knew it was a bad omen.

We planned to set sail in May on favourable tides.

We were ready and well-prepared, but dark days were upon us. A fever and sickness was amongst us. Men, women and children were burning up and dying, but the fever touched only the Tuscarora, and I could sense they blamed us for bringing the illness to their land. The air was now filled with death, sadness and anger.

It was time to leave.

It was early morning when we boarded the boat; we had bid our farewells the night before and were ready to sail. As we rowed away from the beach, I looked back. The sun was now rising, but the sky was filled with black smoke. Beneath the black smoke, a great fire was raging. It was the whole fort and encampment ablaze; everything we had built was now up in flames. The whole Tuscarora tribe were on the beach, yelling, hollering and wailing. They raised up four long poles, on top of which were four heads. They were the heads of Torstein, young Rolf, Flynn and Aidan. Also on the beach, I could now see my wife Sky Bird, her cheeks wet from tears. She held up my son little Thor as if to say, "This will be the last time you will see him." That was now the third time I shed a single tear. I promised myself I would never shed another tear again as nothing could hurt me as much as that single moment in time.

The Tuscarora started to attack us, firing flaming arrows at us and the boat.

"Row fast men, with all your hearts and power!" I ordered.

Red Scar stayed loyal to us, but the three other redskins jumped from the boat and swam back to the beach. We kept rowing until we were safe and out of reach, but Godspeed was badly fire-damaged and a strong wind and current were taking us off course.

We were now heading up the North Coast.

MOHAWK LAND

We needed to repair the boat, so we pulled
into a small cove.

Red Scar warned us, "We are not safe here. This is Mohawk land. Mohawk brutal warriors, much like you Viking."

"In that case," I replied, "Helvin, Toki, Tovi and I will secure the area, while you, Olaf and Dagna repair the boat."

The four of us headed just a small way inland, just enough so we could keep guard from all sides.

Two hours passed slowly, then from out of nowhere, they suddenly appeared before us. Six Mohawks just standing and staring at us. They had never seen anything like us before, and we had never seen anything like them. They had no hair on the sides of their heads, just a band of hair straight down the middle. They had black, hollow, evil-looking eyes and carried spears, clubs and small axes.

"Right, let's do this! Vikings against Mohawks. Let us see who is the mightiest of warriors," said Helvin.

"Fight!" I roared.

With that, Toki and Tovi drew their bows. The Mohawk moved quickly, but the twin's arrows still dropped two of them. Helvin whirled his giant axe, splitting one down the middle. I slashed two of them to pieces with my lightning-fast sword. The last Mohawk had jumped on Toki and was hacking at him with an axe. Tovi took a spear and plunged it into the Mohawk's back until it came out of his stomach.

The Mohawk were dead, but Toki was badly wounded.

Tovi lifted his brother onto his shoulder and we started to make our way back to the boat. After only a couple of paces, more Mohawk came at us, this time about twenty strong. We tried to fight them off but there were too many of them. One Mohawk ran and slid along the ground; as he slid, he hacked at Tovi's legs with an axe. Tovi fell to the ground, dropping his wounded brother. The Mohawk surrounded them both and clubbed them to death with a merciless passion.

"When I say run, Helvin, we turn and run like the wolf. Run!" I shouted.

We both turned and ran like hell back towards the boat, with the Mohawk chasing. As we neared the boat, Dagna came running towards us with a sword in each hand. He ran straight passed us and straight into the chasing Mohawk head on. Dagna went at the Mohawk like a devil-possessed animal, while Helvin and I ran to the safety of the boat. Once on board and safe, we all looked back and witnessed the death of the bravest, craziest man we had ever known.

Dagna died a great warrior's death, taking many Mohawk with him.

As we set off to sea once more, the last sight we saw was that of the Mohawk taunting us. They held aloft the scalps of our friends.

They waved them about in the air, the red hair of the twins and the long, white hair of Dagna. The Mohawk were truly a brutal breed of warrior, and we were glad to see them fade in the distance.

THE JOURNEY HOME

There were now only four of us, but with Olaf's one eye on the stars, he managed to guide us back on course. It was hard going with just the four of us managing the boat, but we kept on going. Days went by, then weeks and then months. We ran out of food, the wind had dropped and the sun was melting us. We had three sharks circling us so we could not fish, and we began to starve. With no energy, we could barely row.

We were slowly dying.

Then one day, without warning, Red Scar stood up, drew a knife and cut his wrists. He looked to the sky, said some words I did not understand and leapt into the sea. We watched in horror as the sharks ripped him to shreds, leaving nothing but blood. After Red Scar's death, the sharks left us alone and once again we could catch fish. Had Red Scar just had enough and given up or had he sacrificed himself to save us? I will never know, but I did know he had been a true friend and I would miss him greatly.

With fish in our bellies, we became strong again but we faced a new problem. Godspeed was letting in water; it was seeping in from all parts of the boat. We had to lighten the load. First, we gave to the sea all of our weapons and shields, even Helvin's great axe. I kept one knife to gut fish, but we were still leaking water. It broke our hearts, but we had to lose the gold to the ocean as well.

Apart from the three of us left, there was no evidence of our great venture. The gold was gone, Red Scar was dead and our fort had been burnt to the ground. All we had left were our hopes of survival and finding our way back home. We had travelled so far – home must now be close.

It was on the calmest of days when, from out of the blue, we were hit by a giant single wave. The wave was as high as the white cliffs of Britain's South Coast. The wave crashed down on us, breaking Godspeed in two. As quickly as it had come, the wave was gone and the sea was calm once more.

I clung onto the boat's broken mast, Helvin swam towards me and also clung onto the mast, but Olaf was nowhere to be seen. I took a deep breath, let go of the mast and swam deep down in search of Olaf. I could see no sign of him. I resurfaced and took another deep breath. I went back under and this time I saw Olaf. He was sinking and struggling to swim up to the surface. I swam down to save him and tried to help him to the surface, but he was weighed down with gold bars. He must have hidden the gold bars on himself when we were throwing them overboard. His one eye and mouth were now both wide open; he was dead. I let Olaf go and he sank deep out of sight. I swam back to the broken mast, which I clung onto, alongside Helvin.

Helvin and I held on tightly and kicked with our feet. We kept kicking until we finally saw land, but try as we might, we could not seem to get close to the shore. It was hot during the day, but nighttime adrift in the sea was freezing cold. I closed my eyes. I could see Sky Bird and little Thor smiling. I must have fallen asleep and been dreaming. I suddenly awoke to bright sunshine burning my eyes, but I was now alone and holding onto the mast by myself.

Helvin must have fallen asleep too, only he must have let go of the mast during the night. The cruel sea had swallowed up my lifelong friend. I broke the promise I had made myself and shed a single tear for my friend whom I loved more than my six brothers and as much as my wife and son.

THE MIRACLE

I was now the last of the ten, the ten men who had set sail from the coast of Ireland on a journey into the unknown. For their memory and honour, I would not be defeated. My feet paddled harder than ever. I must not stop, I must not die, I must make land. I was determined, I was unstoppable and the coastline ahead got closer.

"Arghhh!" I cried out in pain.

A small shark had taken a bite out of my left leg. It came at me again, and this time its sharp teeth tore at my left shoulder. It circled around me, then once more came at me. I let go of the mast and with my right hand, I pulled from my belt the one knife I had kept to gut fish. I struck the knife down on the shark, right between its eyes. The shark wriggled and writhed in a frenzy before swimming away. Blood was draining from my wounds and mixing with the salty seawater. I was not far from shore, but now I had no mast to cling onto. I was treading water, bleeding badly and slowly drowning.

I closed my eyes. I could see the ten of us on Godspeed, laughing and smiling as we began our quest. Then I saw the loving faces of Sky Bird and Little Thor; I saw the heads of Torstein, young Rolf, Aidan and Flynn on top of poles; I saw the red-haired scalps of the twins, Toki and Tovi; I also saw the long white-haired scalp of Dagna. Then I saw the face of Red Scar as he cut his wrists; I saw the open eye of Olaf as he sank into the abyss; then I saw the closed eyes of Helvin, as he let go of the mast.

All this I saw before I was about to drown, but the great God Odin was watching over me and sent a miracle.

I was slowly drowning when a dolphin swam below me and as it rose to the surface. I put my right arm around it and the dolphin pulled me upwards.

I gasped for breath when we emerged into the air. I was alive again! I gently held onto the dolphin as it swam me to the shore. Once in shallow waters, I kissed the dolphin and thanked the Gods. I mustered what little strength I had left and crawled up the beach.

After months at sea, I was on dry land. I dug my fingers into the sand, smiled and passed out. When I finally woke up, I was being cared for by monks in this small monastery.

So now this is the end of my story, which father Benitez has heard and written down. I can only hope Benitez believes my story to be the truth. He must tell the world my story of a new-found land; a land of beauty; a land of Redskin tribes; a land of promise and gold.

For I, Magnus Gunneron, seventh son of a seventh son, must be remembered as a true Viking legend. I must now leave this mortal world and join fellow Viking warriors in the great halls of Valhalla.

The valkyrie carried Magnus to Valhalla. Although he had not died on the battlefield, his life had been one long battle and he was worthy of his place alongside great warriors.

As Magnus entered the halls of Valhalla, he was greeted by his great friend Helvin and the rest of the crew. The ten were once again reunited. Dagna was now with tongue and spoke his first words since he was a child.

"Welcome to Valhalla, dear friend. Come join Viking heroes of the past for you are now a legend and forever immortal."

EPILOGUE

So what happened to Father Benitez and the words he wrote? The words of Magnus and his epic tale? He may have destroyed them, or he may have hidden them in the monastery. He may even have tried to spread the tale across the land; no one knows. Over time, many stories and sagas were told. Some were believed, some not believed, but most were forgotten over the ages.

Some five hundred years later, a man named Christopher Columbus discovered a new world, to great acclaim. Shortly after his discovery, Spanish soldiers were sent to the small monastery.

The Spanish soldiers burnt the monastery to the ground and executed all the monks.

THE END

The
Adventures
of
Scorpio Smith

THE SKELETON'S GOLD

It was 90 degrees in the shade,
yet it was a cold bead of sweat that ran down the
contours of my wrinkled forehead,
reaching the bridge of my nose before sliding into my eye.
This made me squint,
producing a salty teardrop which continued
down the side of my nose
until it reached my dry, scabby, chapped lips.
I licked the droplet from my lips.
It quickly dissolved on my tongue before
I could swallow it
and help soothe my dry parched throat,
which felt like barbed wire had been dragged
up and down it.

I said my prayers and prepared to meet my maker,
under a burning African sun.

My name is William James Smith, but everyone calls me
Scorpio. I was born under that star sign and have a scor-
pion tattooed on both my shoulders. It is 1889 in the year
of our Lord, and Queen Victoria reigns supreme. I am an
archaeologist, explorer, adventurer, treasure hunter, gambler, ex-soldier and one tough bastard son of a bitch. I'm 72
years of age and I have been in Africa for the last 10 years.

Some time ago, when I was excavating near the great
pyramids of Egypt, I came across the bones of a hand pro-
truding from the desert sands. I dug carefully until I had

exposed a fully intact skeleton. In the skeleton's other hand was a leather pouch. Inside, it contained an ancient map and a solid gold bracelet. I put the bracelet on my wrist, I then studied the map. It was in plain black and white, apart from a gold cross on top of what looked like a high plateau. Could this finally be the chance to find gold and the treasures I had spent a lifetime looking for? The skeleton also had a knife stuck in its spine, indicating murder as the cause of death. I buried the skeleton back under the sand, along with the evidence of murder and its unknown past.

I hired 20 bearers and a steamboat. The map led me all along the Nile and into the Congo. We left the boat and cut our way through the jungle until we reached a savannah of sand, rocks and scrub. By this time, I was on my own. My bearers had either been killed or had fled in fear.

By the time I had reached the plateau, I was out of food and water, plus age had caught up with me. There I was, down on my knees and ready to meet my maker under a burning African sun.

THE POWER OF POISON

I was about to die when I thought I heard the sound of water dripping. I mustered up the last of my energy and crawled further along the base of the plateau. I turned a corner and there it was. A strange, yellowish liquid was trickling down the rocky face of the plateau. It looked and smelt disgusting, but I was desperate, so I took the top off my empty water bottle. The top doubled up as a cup, which I filled to the brim. I didn't care if it poisoned me. I just wanted to soothe my razor torn throat. I glugged it down, then another cup and another cup. It was foul.

I must've passed out for a while. It could have been seconds, minutes or hours, I'll never know, but what I do know is I awoke with a new lease of life. I was full of energy and vigour. I drank another cupful, filled up my water bottle with the rank liquid and started the journey back. I was going to need help to climb the plateau and fill my boots with gold.

As I started the journey back, I ran across the dusty savannah, then swung on vines through the jungle until I reached a small, fast-running river. All rivers lead to the Nile, so I lashed myself to a large, broken tree trunk that was stuck on the river bank. I launched myself into the water and drifted down the river.

The current became stronger and stronger. Suddenly I was in rapids. I clung to the tree trunk as it was my only hope of survival. The log kept rolling over, and I kept going under, crashing and smashing into rocks, until I plunged down a waterfall. I was deep under the water with the crashing waves and the mist and the spray of the waterfall above me. I was slowly drowning.

I have no idea how I was able to hold my breath for so long, but I did, and I emerged from the waterfall alive. I drifted down the river until it reached the Nile. Some natives from the Congolese tribe pulled me out of the water and into their canoe. They took me to a riverside mission where a Father O'Connor took me in.

Father O'Connor was a kind soul, originally from County Cork, Ireland. I had my first hot meal in weeks, and the Father shared stories and jokes with me. He also shared a most welcome bottle of brandy. I had a hot bath which had been kindly prepared for me. It was heaven after floating around in dirty, cold water with just a log for company.

It was after a bath, haircut, shave and my first look into a mirror for what seemed like a lifetime that it hit me. It was a miracle! I was no longer a 72-year-old man but a 30-year-old in my prime. The yellow water that had dripped down the rocky face of the plateau was some kind of elixir of life, maybe from a fountain of youth that one hears about in ancient legends.

I knew I had to get back to Cairo and raise some money to fund a new expedition, one that would actually reach the summit of the plateau this time. Father O'Connor arranged for some of the Congolese to paddle me to my hired steamboat, which was luckily still there and ship-shape. The Father also lent me money for supplies and to pay a couple of natives to be crew members. I promised to pay him back tenfold on my return, and I am a man of my word.

THE OASIS

There were only two people in the world that I trusted, my twin sister, Miss Gemini Smith, and my old friend Leo Magee. Gemini was an ex-schoolteacher who, like me, never married or had children. Even though there had been plenty of love affairs for us both, I guess we were both too self-centred for marriage. I had known Leo since school. He was a funny, chubby, little bald man but also very successful and rich. I needed their help, so I telegraphed them when we stopped at the city of Aswan. I asked them to meet me urgently in Cairo. I knew they would leave England as soon as possible and join me in Cairo, and Leo would use his wealth and power to travel as quickly as possible.

When I arrived in Cairo, I booked a suite in the Oasis Hotel. It was the height of luxury, so they had to turn up as I was out of money. Indeed, five days later, they did. As I waited for my guests, I pondered what they would say when they clapped eyes on me. Would they even recognise me, for I was no longer an old man? My rugged good looks had returned, along with my wavy blonde hair. I still had a scar down the right side of my face, which I had received in a knife fight in a Parisian alleyway. My opponents came out of it the worse off though. There were only three of them, so they had no chance against the mighty Scorpio Smith. They were trying to steal my lucky cowboy hat, which I had won in a poker game whilst in New York. I left the three drunken French sailors on their backs, covered in blood and crying out in pain. The rain washed their blood down the gutter and out came the rats. I walked away, stemming the blood flow from my cut cheek with a red bandana that I always wore around my neck. I couldn't leave Paris quickly enough, for it was a cursed hellhole of a city.

There was a knock at the door.

"Entrez vous, my friends! It's good to see you."

They entered the rooms with blank, wide eyed expressions on their faces and disbelief in their eyes. A strange-looking fellow walked in alongside them. He was an American Indian dressed in a red sleeveless shirt, brown leather waistcoat and a bowler hat with a red band and a feather sticking out of it. I poured them each a glass of champagne as I welcomed them in.

"Look here, Scorp, what the hell has happened to you and what the hell is going on?" enquired Gemini.

"Yes, old boy, you've got a lot of explaining to do," added Leo.

"Before I go any further, I need to know who the devil this stranger is, for what I'm about to say must remain a secret between us."

"This is Chief Buffalo Eyes of the Apache tribe," explained Leo. "I call him Taurus. I rescued him from a Wild West show that was playing in London. He was fed up with the way he and the other Indians were being portrayed. So he tried to scalp Buffalo Bill Cody, but as he grabbed Bill's hair, a wig came off in his hand. Then all hell broke loose, with fighting, screaming and yelling.

The crowd were laughing and booing, then throwing whatever they had, fruit and veg, glasses and bottles. The ringmaster sent in the clowns to calm things down, and afterwards, Taurus was kicked out onto the streets. I felt sorry for the poor fellow so I took him in. Since then he has become my aide, my confidante and quite frankly, a dear friend. He doesn't speak much, but when he does, you know his words come from a pure heart. So I trust him more than I do you, and where I go, he goes too, so that's that. Now, Smith, explain yourself!"

I told them everything, then I fetched the water bottle. As we were twins, Gemini was also 72, as was my old school friend Leo. Taurus also looked well into his seventies. I had drunk four cupfuls of the foul yellow water and was now in my thirties. I challenged them to do the same, and who in their right mind would not take up that challenge, with the chance to be in their prime again?

Leo went first, his face grimacing with each cupful. After his fourth cup, he morphed in front of our eyes; he grew younger by the minute until he was in his thirties. Unfortunately for Leo, he was still a funny, chubby, little bald man, but he was happy just to be young again. Next went Taurus. He drank the four cupfuls down with ease, and he, too, became younger in front of us. His wrinkled face was now smooth, his grey hair now as black as a starless night sky, his arms muscular and Herculean. Last was Gemini. She held her nose and downed her four cupfuls. Then, before I could stop her, she poured herself another cup and downed that one too.

"Bugger thirties – I want to be in my twenties!" she declared.

The bottle was now completely empty, and Gemini had transformed into a silky-blonde-haired, blue-eyed, angelic-looking young woman. My twin sister was now my younger sister, but she would no doubt still boss me around.

We spent the rest of the evening laughing, joking and mocking each other. I ordered bottles of the best champagne, Cuban cigars, oysters, steaks and roast chicken. We were having the most wonderful evening when I broke the news that I was penniless and all the hotel bills were in Leo's name. Leo didn't care. He was so happy, and we were all having such a good time that we all burst into joyous laughter.

The next morning after breakfast, I showed them the gold bracelet I was wearing and the map.

Leo started to decipher the map.

"There's not much writing on it, but what there is seems to be in ancient Egyptian hieroglyphics; I would say about 39 B.C. The words next to the golden cross translate as 'the gold of life'."

"How the hell do you know all that?" I asked.

"I have absolutely no idea," said a shocked Leo.

We all vowed to follow the map, climb the plateau and search for the skeleton's gold of life.

We spent the next week hunting down the fastest steamboat we could find. We purchased supplies, guns and ammunition. Taurus visited a market and bought himself a bow, arrows, a small axe and one of the largest knives I had ever seen. Leo bought himself a double-barrelled elephant gun, which was almost as big as him. I stuck with my trusted Smith and Wesson revolver and a Winchester rifle. On one of the cooler days, we went into the desert and practised our newfound skills. For we were not just younger, we were now fitter and stronger. I was always tough and a good gunman, but now I couldn't miss a target. Gemini had learnt a little judo when she was young; now she was an expert in all the martial arts. Taurus was a master with the weapons he had bought from the market, but his greatest weapons were his massive arms. His strength was unnatural but real. Poor Leo was no stronger than before and still a terrible shot, but he had become super intelligent. He seemed to know just about everything. We were now all set for the journey, a journey towards the unknown.

THE JOURNEY

We loaded the boat with all our supplies. It was a fine-looking boat which we were all excited to board. The captain of the boat was Barnaby Jones, a stereotypical old sailor with a striped shirt, white cap, few teeth and a pipe. He had a two-man crew, as well as a cook and a small orphaned African cabin boy called Little Mo. Captain Barnaby Jones liked to be called Skipper, so we all obliged and off we set.

The River Nile twists and turns as it snakes its way through enchanting and dangerous lands. The boat was fast, just as the skipper had promised, and we made great progress. We travelled through Egypt and marvelled at the magical pyramids and ancient ruins that breathed history. Then we journeyed through the Sudan, with its eternal sands of time and marshy river banks. We passed the city of Khartoum at night on the western side of the river, for Khartoum was one of the most dangerous places on earth. Khartoum is situated where the Blue Nile meets the White Nile, a much-valued stronghold. The British-held Khartoum had fallen to the Mahdi Arabs four years ago, and they had killed and beheaded the infamous General Gordon in the process. Khartoum was now a no-go zone for any Europeans. Once we had passed Khartoum, we followed the White Nile into South Sudan.

The majestic Nile was breathtaking, with its eye-bursting sights and regal wildlife. The skies and shores were full of heavenly birds and beasts; our boat cruised past hippos floating obliviously in the African sun.

On a day when the burning sun was scorching more than ever, Little Mo, the African orphan boy, jumped into the river. He was innocently swimming and showing off when two eyes and nostrils rose up from the deep. It was the devil of the Nile, the smiling, razor-toothed crocodile. Mo started panicking, screaming and splashing instead of swimming, with the crocodile getting closer and closer.

I picked up my Winchester rifle and with a steady trigger finger, I shot both of the crocodile's eyes out. Then Taurus pushed passed me, throwing his axe straight between the devil's eyes. Gemini and the skipper pulled Little Mo out of the Nile. He was choking, spluttering and sobbing but alive. Taurus lassoed the monster, then the crew helped him pull the beast onto the boat. Once it was on the boat, the cook began gutting and chopping up the crocodile, for the devil of the Nile was a great food source and his reptilian skin a vital commodity.

We travelled through South Sudan and crossed into the Congo, with its twisted jungles, lakes and waterfalls. The Congo was now called the Congo Free State. It was controlled by Leopold ll's Belgian army. They were there for the rubber plants, which had become a lucrative trade. They were also there for the slave trade, with rumours of them committing hideous atrocities.

THE MISSION

It was our last night on the boat before we reached Father O'Connor's mission, so we all celebrated in the cool evening air under a heavenly African night sky.

"I say, everybody, look what the crew made for me." Leo showed us his new crocodile skin strap for his large elephant gun.

"Well, look what they made me! It's a rather lovely crocodile skin belt, and it certainly brightens up my dull khaki clothes," said Gemini with her hands on her hips, modelling her new belt.

"Me have present too." Taurus showed off a fine-looking necklace made from crocodile teeth.

"What about you, Scorp?" inquired my sister.

I said nothing. I just popped a cigar into my mouth, put a foot on a chair, struck a match on one of my new crocodile boots and lit my cigar. We laughed, teasing each other all through the night. We took turns trying to impress each other. I juggled with knives, Gemini jumped up on the table and did some mid-air somersaults and backflips. Taurus taught Little Mo how to do an Apache war dance, then we tested Leo on his knowledge. We would name a country and he would tell us the capital city. We had to take his word, as none of us knew the answers, but I'm sure he was correct each time as he was a little genius. Then one by one we drifted off to sleep.

In the morning, we arrived at the mission. It was good to be on dry land again. Father O'Connor gave us a warm welcome, and we sat around tables on the decking in front of the mission and ate a hearty breakfast. After breakfast, I paid back the money that the Father had loaned me, not tenfold but fiftyfold. For I was a man of my word and also very generous with Leo's money. The skipper's eyes lit up with raised eyebrows when Father O'Connor brought out some bottles of brandy and we all indulged in brandy coffees. The skipper took his brandy neat. He sat in the shade, chugging away on his pipe, with a gap-toothed smile on his face and a glint in his eyes.

Later on, another expedition turned up. It was led by an English gentleman and a young lieutenant from the British army. The pair joined us on the decking and seemed to know Father O'Connor very well too.

"Henry Morton Stanley, I presume," stated Leo before introducing everyone.

"Why, how do you know who I am, old chap?" replied the English gentleman.

"I have been a great admirer of yours for a long time and have followed your fantastic exploits and discoveries in the British press where you're considered a national hero. I also recognised your fabulous hat that I have seen you wearing in photographs."

Henry wore a British colonial army pith helmet with a white linen scarf wrapped around it and hanging down the back of his neck.

"I say, marvellous observations, old boy. I tell you what, you can have my hat as your head looks like it's getting rather sunburnt; plus, I can easily get a new one."

With that, Henry passed over his pith helmet to Leo, who placed it on his sunburnt head. Leo proudly puffed out his chest and gave a salute.

Henry and the lieutenant sat with us for hours. We listened attentively as Henry told us of the beauty of Lake Victoria, the waterfalls and all the wonders he had witnessed. He told us of his legendary meeting with the great explorer Dr David Livingstone. I stayed very quiet when he told us that the natives were buzzing with rumours of a white apeman who, some months ago, had been spotted swinging through the jungle on vines. While all this was going on, Gemini and the young lieutenant had quietly slipped away unnoticed.

"Gem! Gem! Where are you?" I shouted anxiously.

"It's ok, Scorp, everything's fine," replied my sister as she stepped off the boat with her silky blonde hair looking rather bedraggled.

She was followed by the young lieutenant, who looked like a young man drained of all innocence.

"Just showing the lieutenant our quaint little boat."

The pair re-joined us on the decking with broad, guilty smiles and blushed red faces.

Henry Morton Stanley, the young lieutenant and the rest of their expedition had to depart and continue with their journeys of discovery.

We also had to make plans and pack for our journey, as we would be leaving in the morning at first light.

THE TWISTED JUNGLES

We hired a dozen of the Congolese tribe as our bearers and off we set. We left behind the skipper, Little Mo and the crew in the safe hands of Father O'Connor. They would wait with the boat at the mission for hopefully our safe return and the treasurers we sought.

We followed the map, carving our way through the jungle with machetes. Unlike me, Leo could read the map properly. When I had discovered the plateau, it was by luck. I remember going round in circles, getting lost and almost dying on my knees. The map showed a tall tree that had been struck by lightning. When we found the tall tree, it was in a small clearing. The clearing was a perfect spot to rest up, so we set up tents and lit a campfire. Six days had passed, and according to the map, we were about halfway through the jungle and all was well.

Nighttime came and the four of us were around the campfire discussing the next leg of the journey when we sensed an unease amongst the bearers. Suddenly we heard a deathly scream. One of the bearers who had earlier deserted us came staggering back into the camp. He dropped down dead right in front of our eyes, his body covered in claw marks.

"Anyoto! Anyoto! Anyoto!" shouted the bearers with fear in their voices.

"What the hell are they shouting about, Leo?" I asked as I picked up my rifle.

"The Anyoto are a tribe of cannibals also known as the Leopard Men. They dress in leopard skins and carry short spears with claws on the end," answered Leo as he picked up his large elephant gun.

All the bearers fled for their lives. They ran into the jungle, blinded by fear. Every now and again, we would hear their cries of death. We stood back to back facing all directions. The twisted jungle was now full of staring eyes. The Leopard Men came at us with their clawed spears, but they were no match for the four of us. I faced them head-on with a rifle in one hand and pistol in the other. Gemini took out the ones on the left, firing bullet after bullet. On the right, Taurus fired arrow after arrow. They attacked us from behind, but Leo was ready for them. Leo fired both barrels of his elephant gun, blasting the Leopard Men, chopping them down like trees, but the recoil of the elephant gun kicked Leo backwards. Leo ended up flat on his back in the ashes of the campfire. The fight came to an end. The Leopard Men lay dead or crawling back into the jungle. We pulled Leo up onto his feet and dusted him down.

"Well, I do declare that was a frightfully exciting experience! Did you see how many I took out with my gun? Jolly good show, I say, jolly good show," blustered Leo as he puffed out his chest.

We spent the rest of the night huddled round the campfire. None of us slept as we waited for the morning sun to rise.

Morning had broken, and once more we set off through the jungle. The four of us could travel more quickly without the Congolese bearers, and we made good headway. After a couple of days, we reached the next point on the map. It was a waterfall that thundered down into a small stream. I set up the tents while Leo and Taurus gathered firewood. Meanwhile, Gemini went for a dip in the stream.

Gemini stood before me, dripping wet and teary-eyed. A Belgian officer had one hand around her throat and one hand on a pistol that was pointed at her head. He was backed up by four young soldiers, nervously pointing their guns. I was now backed up by Leo and Taurus, who had returned from gathering wood. Leo aimed his elephant gun at the nervous-looking young soldiers. Taurus pulled out his axe and large knife, twirling them with menace.

The Belgian officer spoke in English. "I am Captain De Bruyne of Leopold ll's Belgian army. You must be the famous Scorpio Smith, and this young lady I hold captive must be your sister, Miss Gemini Smith. There are no secrets in Africa but plenty of rumours, and rumour has it you are following a treasure map. Now all you have to do is hand me the map and then I will let your sister go. It's as simple as that because I hold all the cards."

I calmly replied, "You may hold all the cards, but I'm a gambler who always has an ace up his sleeve. The problem is that you forgot about the other Smith, Smith 'n' Wesson!"

Before the officer could blink or twitch, I drew my revolver and shot off his trigger finger. Gemini quickly spun around, kicked him in the groin and karate chopped him in the neck. The officer lay on the ground in agony, his hand spurting blood profusely. The four soldiers froze with fear and shock but still pointed their guns.

"Looks like we have ourselves a Mexican stand-off, and I don't fancy your chances much. So if I were you, I would get back to your company, drag captain De Bruyne with you and forget you ever saw us because no one messes with my sister. So move on and don't look back."

The Belgians could see how fast I was with a gun. They also didn't like the look of Leo's elephant gun with both barrels pointing at them. And they had never seen an Apache Red Indian before. In fact, I don't think most of Africa had seen one before. Taurus flashed his large knife at them, and they backed away into the jungle.

We would never see them again.

THE PLATEAU

We came out of the jungle and into the savannah. We could see the plateau far in the distance. The savannah was a mix of trees, rocks, scrubland, grass and dust. We trekked through the savannah at a fast pace, for we had an unbelievable amount of stamina and boundless energy. As we made our way to the plateau, we passed an array of stunning wildlife. We witnessed herds of antelope, elephant and rhino, all foraging for food. We saw hyenas scavenging, cheetahs running, lions hunting and vultures picking at carcasses. Hundreds of animals fighting for survival in their beautiful but harsh, godforsaken land. The closer we got to the plateau, the more formidable and foreboding it looked as it rose high into the African sky.

After a couple of days of trekking across the savannah, we reached the base of the plateau. It was early morning, so we had some breakfast and then started circling the plateau. We turned a corner and there it was: the spot where I had nearly died, but now there was no yellow water dripping down the rock face. All that was left was a dried-up yellowish stain that went all the way up the rocky face, right to the very top.

We all looked at each other with defeated eyes.

Then Gemini smiled and enthused, "Cheer up, everyone! Just because it's dried up on the rock face, it doesn't mean there isn't any more at the top. Plus there might be more gold like the bracelet and all sorts of treasures and wonders up there."

"Gem's right," I said. "Let's finish what we started. Let's climb this damn plateau. After all, we're supposed to be adventurers, aren't we?"

"Hear, hear. Bravo!" added Leo.

Taurus just nodded his head approvingly before announcing, "I will climb. Give me rope."

Taurus began scaling the rock face with his hands, gripping the jagged rocks like a vice, and his strong powerful arms pulled him up. Higher and higher, up and up he climbed. He had no fear, but we feared for his life. Finally, he reached the top. He tied the rope to a large tree stump and lowered it down to us. One by one, we climbed the rope until we were all at the top of the rock face. We were now on a large ledge with just a few rocks and trees on it. We followed the yellow stain, which led us into a dome-shaped cave. The cave had a hole in its roof which let in the sunlight. The sun lit up the cave to reveal a large boulder in the middle. Built into the top of the boulder was a giant marble wok-shaped dish. However, the dish was empty, just badly stained and cracked. The gold of life had leaked through the crack and trickled out of the cave and down the rocky face of the plateau.

I must have got lucky all those months ago when I was down on my knees dying. It was a miracle that the yellow liquid had saved my life. I guess I was just in the right place at the right time, and when I had filled up my water bottle, it was with the last drops of the gold of life.

At the other end of the cave was another opening. We made our way through to another large ledge. There was a ravine below us, and in front of us was a man-made bridge of wooden slats and ropes. We walked nervously across the bridge to the other side. On the other side was a vast mystical land, a beautiful new horizon, a landscape full of wonder.

THE QUEEN AND GODDESS

As we made our way through the land, we saw that some of it had been cultivated. There were fields of cotton, corn and wheat. There were plots of vegetables and orchards of fruit. As we headed to what looked like a small, half-built pyramid, we were suddenly surrounded by thirty-odd spears in the hands of what looked like Egyptians. There were too many of them to fight, so we let them lead us to their village.

Their village was a large encampment of wooden houses. It had a crystal clear stream running through it, and at the end of the village stood the small half-built pyramid. The Egyptians jabbed their spears at us, herding us towards the pyramid. Before the pyramid was a marble throne. Sat upon the throne was the most beautiful woman the world had ever seen. Her hair was as black as coal, her lips flaming red, she had ivory toned skin and her charcoal-lined eyes sparkled like diamonds.

Leo spoke in astonishment. "Surely, she can't possibly be, can she, the queen of Egypt, Cleopatra? But she committed suicide in 39 B.C. Mind you, they never did discover her body or tomb."

Cleopatra was famous for speaking many languages, and now so could my friend Leo. Leo began to interrogate the Queen in Latin, then translated it back to us. The Queen told us her tale of death, life and miracles.

"Yes, I am Queen Cleopatra, the Egyptian Goddess."

"The love of my life, Mark Anthony, had committed suicide and my empire was collapsing all around me. I was contemplating suicide myself, as I had nothing left to live for, when I remembered my people; I had to live for them. I gathered together my royal guard, my most loyal subjects, my handmaids, the high priest and as much of my riches as we could carry. We faked my death and escaped into the night on a sailboat.

"We took the long journey down the Nile into darkest Africa. We were going where no civilised people had gone before. The native savages would bow down before me as if they somehow knew I was a goddess. It was when I saw the plateau that I realised what our destiny would be. I had to lead my people to the top and hide us away from the rest of the world.

"We found a steep pathway that led us up to the top of the plateau. Then we started an avalanche of boulders and rocks to block the pathway and stop anyone from finding us. We began building new homes and a new future for ourselves. The years went by and I grew old and ugly.

"We discovered a cave on the other side of a small ravine. I ordered a bridge to be built to reach the other side. Once the bridge was finished, I walked across the bridge. Then I and I alone entered the cave. As soon as I saw the golden water in the marble dish, I knew it was heaven-sent from the gods. I drank the gold of life from the dish, and when I reappeared from the cave, I was young and beautiful again.

"I was now an immortal Queen and Goddess. I forbade anyone else from entering the cave with the punishment of death.

"But the high priest betrayed me; he drugged the guards and entered the cave. The high priest then escaped from the plateau to return to Egypt and tell all who would listen about the plateau and the gold of life. On discovering his betrayal, I sent one of my royal guards to hunt down the traitor.

"The guard finally caught up with the high priest in Egypt and stabbed the traitor in the back before burying him in the desert.

"Two hundred years passed and I started to grow old again, so I re-entered the cave and once more drank the gold of life from the marble dish. I continued doing this every two hundred years, but while I stayed immortal, my people grew old and died and new generations followed on.

"I knew one day that the gold of life would run dry, so that's why I ordered the building of the pyramid. When I die, I will be entombed inside with all my riches.

"Many months ago, I went into the cave and saw that the dish was cracked and leaking. I drank the last drops of the gold of life and now have only two hundred years or so to live. Two hundred years is a short time when you have already lived for nearly two thousand."

Leo told Cleopatra our story of how we had reached the plateau and assured her that when we left we would tell no one of what we had seen. Her secrets would be safe with us.

Cleopatra looked up to the sky and then looked down upon us. She ordered her men to disarm us before having us thrown into the pyramid. Her men then imprisoned us in the pyramid by pushing a giant bolder against the entrance.

The Queen couldn't risk us leaving, so we were to be locked inside the pyramid until a funeral pyre was built. Then we would be sacrificed to her gods.

THE GREAT ESCAPE

Nighttime came and the four of us were trapped inside the pyramid. As strong as Taurus was, he couldn't budge the boulder that blocked the entrance. We could find no other way out. The half-built walls were too smooth to climb and the tops of the walls just out of reach. The only light we had was from the African stars and a full moon shining down on us. In one of the corners we had found Cleopatra's riches. There were Roman coins, gold jewellery, diamonds, rubies and pearls. All these riches were to be entombed with Cleopatra when she eventually died. What a waste, but all this treasure was of no use to us; we were imprisoned and awaiting our deaths.

Finally, I had an idea.

"Listen up – I've got a plan to get us out of here. Taurus and I will squat down and clasp our hands. Then Gem will put one foot in each of our hands and Taurus and I will spring up and fling Gem into the air. Then Gem can grab the top of the wall, pull herself up and climb down the outside walls of the pyramid."

"What happens next?" asked Gemini.

"Well, the rest is up to you, sis. I'm sure you'll think of something – you always do. Besides, has anyone else got a better idea?"

"Let's do this," said Taurus.

Leo counted us down, "1, 2, 3 go!"

Gemini screamed as we launched her into the air. "Whoooaaarh!"

We caught her as she fell back down and tried again.

"Higher this time. 1, 2, 3 go!"

"Whoooaaarh!"

"Come along, chaps, put your backs into it. 1, 2, 3 go!"

"Whoooaaarh!"

This time, Gemini grabbed the top of the wall and pulled herself up.

"Back soon, darlings. Make sure you don't go anywhere," and off she went.

Gemini climbed down the outside walls of the pyramid and reached the bottom safely, but there were two guards waiting for her. Gemini quickly drop-kicked one in the head, then threw the other one over her shoulder, smashing him against the pyramid wall. They were both knocked out cold.

It was late at night and the rest of the Egyptians were fast asleep. Gemini snuck around the village in the dark until she came across our belongings. She took one of our ropes and as many of our weapons as she could carry, then made her way back to the top of the pyramid wall and lowered down the rope inside.

"I'm back, boys! Have you missed me?"

"Just hold onto the goddamn rope, Gem," I shouted, trying not to laugh.

Gemini held on tight as one by one we climbed up the rope.

"What about the treasure? We've all forgotten about the treasure! That's what we came here for."

Leo was right, but we had no time to go back. We had to escape and the sun was about to rise.

We gathered up our weapons. Gemini had managed to retrieve a couple of rifles, my Smith and Wesson revolver, Leo's elephant gun and Taurus's large knife and axe. We filled our water bottles with water from the crystal-clear stream then made our way out of the village.

We headed back towards the bridge and the cave. Suddenly there were arrows flying all around us. The Egyptians were chasing after us. We ran as fast as we could, dodging arrows and spears. We made it to the bridge, but Leo had lagged behind. He fell to the ground when an arrow struck him in the back.

"Cross the bridge. I will go back for him. Go now! Go!" shouted Taurus.

Gemini and I crossed the wooden bridge to the ledge on the other side and took cover behind some rocks. Taurus went back for Leo. In a single move, he swooped Leo up and tossed him onto his shoulder. He carried him onto the bridge and was halfway across when two arrows struck him, one arrow stuck in his shoulder and the other arrow pierced his thigh, but he still managed to stagger across the bridge.

Gemini attended to Leo and Taurus while I covered them, firing my rifle until I ran out of bullets. The Egyptians had never seen or heard a gun being fired before, so they started to back away. I was reloading my gun when we heard the drone of long horns being blown. Cleopatra arrived and fearlessly walked towards the bridge. All her royal guards came to stand alongside her. She ordered one of her guards to cut the ropes that secured the bridge. The guard drew out a short sword and began cutting the ropes.

Cleopatra wanted the bridge to be cut down so no one could cross again. I put down my rifle, borrowed Taurus's large knife and began cutting the ropes on our side of the bridge. It was my way of saying we were never coming back and that she and her people would remain safe from the outside world. The bridge collapsed falling down into the ravine. Cleopatra understood my gesture. She raised her arm up to the African sun, then all her guards raised their spears and saluted us. I took off my lucky cowboy hat, held it to my heart and saluted her back. Cleopatra was truly the most beautiful woman the world had ever seen, a goddess and a great queen.

I wondered what would become of them all. I imagined they would finish building the pyramid and in a couple of hundred years time, entomb Cleopatra with all her riches. Maybe in generations to come, they would venture down from the plateau and join the rest of civilisation. Who knows?

We pulled the arrows out of our wounded friends, and right before our eyes, their wounds healed, leaving small scars. They both stood up and we all embraced each other with warm affection. We made our way back through the cave, passing the empty, gold-stained marble dish with remorse as to what could have been. One by one, we climbed back down the rocky face of the plateau.

HOMEWARD BOUND

We sat at the base of the plateau, exhausted and speechless, until Leo broke the silence.

"I say, chaps, that was a frightfully exciting adventure, was it not, but we have nothing to show for it! No gold of life, no riches, just empty pockets."

Then Gemini piped up, "Speak for yourself. My pockets aren't empty."

With that, Gemini stood up and emptied her trouser pockets, her back pockets and all her jacket pockets. Out came handful after handful of Roman coins, gold jewellery, rubies, diamonds and pearls.

"Bloody hell, Gem!" I shouted in shock. "No wonder it took us three attempts to fling you up that goddamn wall. I thought you had just put on a few pounds."

"You know me. I never could resist a bit of sparkle."

We all marvelled at the stolen treasure that lay before us. We were now rich beyond our dreams. I stood up before my friends and made an impassioned speech.

"Listen up. We've all been given a gift, a gift we cannot waste. We have two hundred years ahead of us, living in peak condition and in the prime of our lives. Let us not waste these years. Let us take this opportunity to help the poor and needy. We can use our skills to seek out riches from all four corners of the world. Any treasure we find we will sell and use the money for good causes. We will become treasure-hunting crusaders, the unsung heroes from the secret gold of life."

"Hear, hear! Jolly good show, I say," blustered Leo.

"Count me in," said Taurus in his usual blunt manner.

After some umming and ahing, Gemini agreed too.

"Oh, alright then. As long as I can keep the odd piece of jewellery, you can count me in."

With that, we all shook hands and made a vow to live our lives to the full.

We trekked back through the savannah and the jungle until we reached the mission. It was good to be back amongst friends again. We stayed at the mission for a couple of days, relaxing and enjoying ourselves. Then we were back on the boat again with the skipper, his crew and Little Mo. Before we left, I gave Father O'Connor all the rubies, for there was no better man than Father O'Connor to make good use of them.

We journeyed once more along the Nile and into Cairo. We were sad to leave our friends on the boat. We would all miss them and remember them with much love. As we said our goodbyes, I handed all of the Roman coins to the skipper, and Barnaby Jones promised to help more orphans like Little Mo.

ENGLAND

We sailed across the Mediterranean, rode trains across Europe, then took a boat across the English Channel. We travelled in a horse-drawn carriage until we reached Leo's country estate. His manor house would become our new home. We passed the diamonds on to the local hospitals and the pearls to the poorhouses. We kept the gold jewellery to finance our next adventure, apart from the odd piece that Gemini picked for herself. It seemed only fair. After all, she was the one who had filled her pockets, and she does love a bit of sparkle.

It was good to be back in England. I had been away for so long I'd forgotten how much I missed and loved my country. The hills, the valleys, the forests, the green grass and the flowers. The sights, the smells, the rain, the people and above all the pride in being an Englishman. We have our queen, too. She may not be beautiful like Cleopatra, but Queen Victoria is truly a great queen. I wondered when the four of us would set off again and to what part of the world our next adventure would take us.

One thing I did know was that no matter where I went, I would always be an Englishman and England would always be my home.

The End

The

SPEAR

INTRODUCTION

This is a tale of three births, legends and deaths.
The births of Jesus, Barabbas and a Roman spear.
The parallel legends of Jesus and his miracles
against Barabbas and his murders.
He, in turn, is hunted down by a Roman soldier,
Marcus Vittori,
the possessor of the spear, that will become
the Spear of Destiny.

THREE BIRTHS

The year zero. In a dark blue sky shines the brightest star the world has ever seen. Below, the birth of Jesus, the son of Mary and the son of God. Born in a barn but adored by kings.

No one adored Barabbas, the bastard son of a whore (some say the son of Satan), born in the gutter.

The star never shone over Barabbas.

The spear born straight and true. A typical Roman spear, designed for battle, to maim and kill in the hands of a young soldier.

Marcus Vittori.

THE LEGENDS BEGIN

Some thirty years later, Marcus is no longer a young soldier but an old, battle-worn centurion, with the spear still in hand.

His face was a map of scars and wrinkles. It was weather-beaten and rugged, but it was still a strikingly handsome face. He had a sparkle in his eyes which was pure and honest. But that sparkle could turn into a stare that could cut like a knife. He was six foot of muscle and power, as tough as leather and as hard as granite. And all those who saw him fight would deem him,

indestructible.

As a centurion, Marcus Vittori was in command of a unit of highly trained men. But he had lost forty-four of his men fighting in the Roman-Germanic wars. They had spilled their blood from the Rhine to the Elba. After years of fighting and years of patrolling borders, their campaign was over. They were the last of their legion to be sent back home to Rome. They had been tough years, but they were nearly at an end. All roads lead to Rome, but this road had been long and hard and was not quite over.

They woke to a beautiful day, had breakfast and broke camp. Marcus looked up at the cloudless blue sky. He noticed a magnificent eagle floating on the cool breeze, occasionally flapping its incredibly wide wings. The sunlight suddenly hit the spear, and the point shone like a diamond. Marcus saw this as some kind of omen.

"There's a storm coming men – prepare for battle," he warned.

The enemy approached from the north. They were a renegade Germanic tribe, thirsty for Roman blood and outnumbering the Romans three to one. Marcus barked out his orders as the enemy attacked.

"Up shields and hold your lines."

The enemy threw everything at them – spears, arrows, axes and rocks.

"Back ten paces and keep formation."

The Roman army was the best the world had seen, but this small unit was in dire trouble.

"Fall back twenty paces. Keep your shields up and your hearts strong."

Their shields were starting to splinter and break up. Marcus spotted the tribe's chieftain in the distance on a white horse. He broke from the formation, ran sideways through a hail of arrows and scaled a rocky mound. Once on top, for a short moment, it felt as though time had frozen and there was a deathly silence.

Marcus launched the spear with all his power, piercing the sky for a distance never thrown before. It finally reached its destination, the Adam's apple of the enemy chief. In that instant, the enemy tribe lost all courage.

Marcus drew his sword and held it aloft, pointing skyward.

He yelled out, "For Caesar and Rome!" before running down towards his foe.

His men echoed his battle cry: "For Caesar and Rome! For Caesar and Rome!"

They broke formation and charged the enemy with an unstoppable bravado.

The leaderless tribe had no stomach for the fight that was now upon them. The Romans cut, slashed and slaughtered their way through them all, for they did have the stomach for the fight and were hungry for it. Within half an hour, the battle was over and the victory Roman.

The green grass was splattered with blood, and bodies lay all around. Some missing limbs, some missing heads. The Romans had totally decimated their enemy, with the loss of only nine men. But they were nine of their band of brothers never to reach home. They buried the nine men and left the enemy corpses to the wolves.

Marcus retrieved the spear from the Chieftain's throat and cleaned it so that it would once again shine like a diamond in the sunlight. As he did so, the eagle he had seen earlier flew down onto the dead Chieftain's chest and began pecking out his eyes.

Marcus promised the rest of his men he would get them all home safely without any more loss, and he did. Marcus returned to Rome a hero and his spear renowned and infamous. But he had seen too much battle and now yearned for peace. As a reward, Marcus was sent to a quiet Roman outpost,

Jerusalem.

THE DEVIL

Jesus knew he had a destiny and left behind his quiet life. He went into the wilderness to fast, and after rejecting the Devil's temptations, he returned from the wilderness to start his mission in life. As he spoke the word of God, disciples followed and crowds would gather.

Barabbas never rejected the Devil but embraced him. Abandoned by his mother as a child, he had grown up on the streets, a feral beggar, next becoming a slave for over ten years.

He was evil personified, with dark hair, dark eyes and a black heart. His toned body was covered in lash scars from all the whippings he had received. He had an extraordinary pain threshold and would just look his oppressors in the eye and grin insanely.

There was a full moon in a black velvet sky on the night Barabbas made his escape from bondage. He had spent over three hours chewing through the rope that tethered him, only stopping to puke or spit out blood. Once free, he scuttled away like a rat. But before he escaped there was one thing he had to do.

Barabbas sneaked into his master's quarters, stole his sword and stuck it into his bloated belly. His master's eyes opened wide, but he could not cry out; he could only gurgle blood. Barabbas twisted the sword and sniggered under his breath as he watched him die.

This was his first killing, but it was not to be his last. He escaped into the dark shadows of the moonlight. He now had the stench of blood and the shadow of death upon him.

And he loved it.

CASSIUS

Marcus and a young soldier, Cassius Longinus, had been assigned the task of hunting down and capturing Barabbas, the escaped slave and murderer.

Although Cassius was young, he was ambitious and intelligent. This was to be his first mission as the only action he had seen before was fighting off women and running from their husbands. His boyish charms, blue eyes and curly blonde hair would dizzy girls' minds and melt their hearts. As a soldier, he yearned for experience and craved adventure. The hunt for Barabbas would certainly supply both.

They headed north on horseback to a place called Bethel, from where Barabbas had escaped. They heard rumours from his fellow slaves that he would head further north to Tiberius, the city where he used to beg. Marcus and Cassius began the long journey north. During the hunt, they would become good loyal friends.

Cassius knew all about the spear and bravery of Marcus Vittori; he looked up to him with high regard and great respect. Cassius was keen and eager to learn, and at every opportunity, he would get Marcus to train him to fight, for Cassius longed to be a great Roman warrior. Marcus took Cassius under his wing like the son he had never had. It wasn't long before Barabbas would leave a trail of blood for them to follow.

THE CRIPPLE

Barabbas had been on the run for many days, when he came across a shepherd boy tending his flock.

"Hey, boy," said Barabbas, "I need meat. I'm going down the hill to slaughter one of your flock. I suggest you stay where you are."

Barabbas started down the hill, but the boy ran in front and confronted him.

"I can't let you do that! Here, please take this bread instead," begged the boy.

Barabbas slapped the boy to the ground, picked up the boy's crook and repeatedly smashed it down on the boy's legs, again and again until it snapped, just like the boy's legs.

"Now, boy, I suggest you stay where you are this time," Barabbas said sarcastically.

He proceeded down the hill and slaughtered a lamb.

Marcus and Cassius came across a Bedouin encampment. They were welcomed and watered their horses. There was a sadness in the air and a lot of sorrowful faces. They were shown to a tent where a grieving mother was tending her crippled son. The brave shepherd boy gave them a description of his attacker. They knew it was Barabbas and explained how they were hunting him down. They promised them all they would either capture him or kill him. They spent the night at the camp before leaving at the crack of dawn.

As Jesus and his disciples roamed the land, word of his miracles spread far and wide.

Jesus had cured a cripple; Barabbas crippled a shepherd just for food.

THE STONING

Barabbas had been walking and running for miles when he chanced upon a small farm, just east of a town called Sychar.

"I need water," gasped Barabbas.

The farmer who greeted him was an old man in his twilight years.

"Help yourself, friend, and take what you want," said the farmer.

"I'm not your friend, but I will take what I want, and I want your best horse," replied Barabbas.

The old man shook as he spoke. "I'm afraid that's not possible. Will you please go now?"

Barabbas picked up a rock and calmly struck it against the old man's head. The farmer collapsed on the ground, shaking even more as blood escaped from his skull.

"I am Barabbas, and anything and everything is possible," he declared before leaving the old man to die.

The spear seemed to guide Marcus on the hunt for Barabbas, and its power had led them to the farm. When they came across the farmer, buzzards were devouring his flesh. They now knew Barabbas was no longer on foot but on a fresh horse. Sickened by the sight before them, they wasted no time and rode off, following his tracks before the sun set.

Jesus had stopped the stoning of Mary Magdalene; Barabbas cracked open the skull of a farmer with a rock just for fresh water and a horse.

THE LEPER

Barabbas had reached a town called Nain. Having taken his fill of food and wine, he craved sex. He bedded a local whore who went by the name of Helena. She had satisfied all of his needs and demands, but when Helena asked for payment, the mood changed. Barabbas flew into a dark red rage, shouting at her,

"I don't pay, but you will pay, you dirty bitch whore."

He then proceeded to gag, rape, whip and beat her.

Barabbas left Helena a weeping, broken mess on the floor, like a trampled flower in the rain crying for sunshine. He took with him all her jewellery and stole what money she had, for this maniac had no conscience.

By the time Marcus and Cassius arrived in the town of Nain, it was too late. Helena could not look at her face in the mirror, and with no money and unable to work, she had hanged herself.

Jesus had cured a leper of scabs and sores; Barabbas raped and beat a woman, leaving her covered in cuts and bruises and disfigured for life.

THE BLIND MAN

Barabbas had trekked around Mount Tabor and was heading towards Tiberius when he came across a travelling merchant. The sun was setting and the merchant had set up camp for the night.

"God be with you, stranger. Please join me by the fire. Sit down and rest and I will cook food for us to share. They call me Tarko, the fat one," welcomed the merchant.

"God is not with me, but I am cold, tired and hungry, so I will join you," replied Barabbas.

The two men huddled round the fire and shared food under the chilly night stars.

Tarko spoke of his travels across different countries and of his great trading powers. He told of buying and selling anything and everything from jewellery to spices, from pots and pans to fine satins and silks.

Tarko was suddenly speechless and froze with fear. A deadly snake slithered towards them, hissing with menace. The snake struck like lightning, sinking its fangs deep into the ankle of Barabbas. But within seconds, the snake was dead, poisoned by the blood of Barabbas. Without flinching, Barabbas picked up the dead serpent, kissed its face and laughed before tossing it onto the fire. The snake hissed even louder as its skin sizzled on the fire.

"I have seen many sights in my time but nothing quite like that before. I bid you goodnight, Barabbas, the snake kisser," said Tarko before he drifted off to sleep.

Barabbas slept with one eye open. He had spied a large purse of coins tied onto one of Tarko's donkeys.

Barabbas slept through the night with an evil smile on his snaked kissed lips.

Barabbas woke early to the sound of Tarko grunting and snoring. He took the purse of coins and tied it to his own horse. Barabbas was about to mount his horse when he felt a tap on his shoulder. He turned round to find an angry Tarko with a staff in his hands.

"Give me back my purse, then be on your way. I never want to lay eyes on you again," demanded Tarko.

"Don't worry, you won't see me again, you fat, grunting pig," retorted Barabbas.

Tarko swung the staff at Barabbas, but he was too quick and ducked… As Barabbas sprung back up, he head-butted Tarko and kneed him in the groin. He pushed him onto the smouldering fire, then pinned him down. Barabbas stuck his thumbs into Tarko's eyes, grinning insanely as he blinded him.

Barabbas left Tarko rolling in the ashes and screaming in extreme agony. He rode off with not only the large purse of coins but also Tarko's donkeys laden with fine goods.

When the two Roman hunters came across the merchant, he was stone-cold dead. The blind Tarko had crawled out of the fire and into a nearby nest of vipers. The sight of his body tortured by the snakes was swollen and discoloured. The two men quickly rode off and headed for the city of Tiberius.

Jesus had cured a blind man; Barabbas blinded a merchant for a purse of coins.

THE HUNT

Tiberius was a bustling city near the beautiful Sea of Galilee. Barabbas had intended on settling down in Tiberius, but the streets where he once grew up had brought back bad memories. Also, the thought of his mother still living there turned his stomach. He soon sold on all of Tarko's wares and his donkeys in the market places. He was now a wealthy man and had heard that Jerusalem was the city for him. Barabbas left Tiberius and headed south along the river Jordan towards Jerusalem.

The hunt for Barabbas had taken Marcus and Cassius all across Judea and Samaria. They were harsh, rugged and mountainous territories, with cold nights and hot days. Some days were so hot it felt as if their bodies could melt, like iron in a blacksmith's furnace. Along the way, they had endured hunger, thirst, scorpions, rats, snakes and a sandstorm that had nearly buried them alive.

But they had also witnessed much beauty, such as the awe-inspiring Mount Tabor and the beautiful Sea of Galilee, where they had spent a morning bathing in its turquoise waves. And now they were heading south along the majestic River Jordan.

They were never far behind Barabbas, but each time they found a victim, a day behind felt like a week and a mile behind felt like a hundred.

Cassius had never witnessed such evil and brutality before. Disgusted, he vowed to see Barabbas draw his last breath.

Marcus had seen plenty of evil and brutality before. He had killed many himself, but that was the blood of war; this was the blood of Hades.

During the hunt, the words and miracles of Jesus had reached Marcus. They resonated with him: humanity, peace, love, compassion and forgiveness. To do unto others as you would have done to yourself. These words gave Marcus hope and a dream of a better life, a better world, an escape from the horror that was surrounding him, and maybe even a better future. Until such time, it was the spear that guided him, and the hunt was on.

RHINOCE

The two tired Romans stopped at a small, dusty town called Pella.

"Cassius, there's a tavern over there. Go inside and order some food while I tend to the horses," said Marcus.

Cassius went inside but came out quicker than he had entered. He came out through the air before sliding on his backside along the dusty ground. He was spread-eagled on his back and out cold. Cassius was then followed out by a Goliath of a man, over 350lbs, wrapped in a skin as black as the night sky.

"Hey! Roman dog, take your friend and go, unless you want a piece of me. I am Rhinoce, champion of the River Jordan," bellowed the giant black man.

"I do not seek trouble, but I also never run from it. My advice to you is to move aside, big man," replied Marcus.

Rhinoce laughed until he saw the icy chill in Marcus's cold hard stare.

The two men locked eyes and then locked horns as they began to wrestle. Rhinoce was twice the size, but Marcus was fast and agile. They both grappled hard and furious. Their bodies intertwined and knotted, they were both locked together on the ground, choking each other.

"Roman dog, release your grip and I will let you live," gasped Rhinoce.

"No, you release your grip first. I am quite comfortable lying here, and eventually my friend will awake and kill you," croaked Marcus.

"Ha! I like you, Roman. I could stay here forever, but I am thirsty for wine. Today you are lucky, and I will let you live." Rhinoce loosened his grip.

"Well, I will also let you live, so we will call it a friendly draw and go drink until we drop," Marcus replied with a smile.

Both men laughed as they stood up and dusted each other down. Marcus took a bucket of water and sloshed it over Cassius.

"Urgh, what happened?" moaned Cassius as he came to.

"You were kicked by an ass," laughed Marcus.

The tavern was full of life and laughter. Men sang and women danced and everyone drank. Cassius charmed the women, while Marcus and Rhinoce shared wine and stories.

"Rhinoce is a strange name. How did you come by it?" enquired Marcus.

"It was from when I lived in Africa," began Rhinoce. "I was a young man of about twenty. I was out hunting with my father and two brothers; we had caught an antelope and were on our way home when suddenly this huge monster called a rhinoceros charged at us. My father shouted at us to run for cover. But me being so big, strong, brave and stupid, I charged back at the monster. Naturally, I came off the worse, my shield shattered, and I was flung to kingdom come. But I lived to tell the tale, and have been called Rhinoce ever since."

"Sounds like a friendly draw to me," joked Marcus.

Both men charged their bottles and roared with laughter.

Out of the corner of his eye, Marcus spotted Cassius slipping out of the door with two young women he had worked his charm on. Marcus smiled to himself and turned back to Rhinoce, but he was now asleep on the floor.

A soft voice whispered in his ear, "You look tired too. Come home with me and you will have a warm bed and a massage you will never forget."

Marcus turned to face a good-looking middle-aged woman who went by the name of Olivia. He kissed her soft pillow lips as he gazed into her glowing eyes. This was an offer he could not refuse.

Olivia did indeed give Marcus a massage he would never forget. It had been a long time since he had shared a bed with a woman, so he made the most of this opportunity. He made love to Olivia all night long, penetrating her again and again.

The morning came and the sun rose in the sky, giving warmth to the cool air. The two Romans met up by their horses outside the tavern.

"You have a good night?" asked Marcus.

"A very good night. I'm tired, though – I only got an hour's sleep," replied Cassius.

"Mmmm," smirked Marcus, "that's more than I got."

They both smiled as they mounted their horses. An eagle flew above them, casting a shadow, heading south. Then their eyes were briefly dazzled by the sunlight as it hit the spear.

"I know where he's going – Barabbas goes south to Jerusalem. Come, let's ride!" ordered Marcus.

"Jerusalem, good, it will be good to get back; my arse can't take much more of this horse," replied a bleary-eyed Cassius.

As they rode off, a stumbling, hungover Rhinoce shouted at them.

"Hey! Roman dogs, good luck and God be with you, and stay clear of monsters."

JERUSALEM

Jesus entered Jerusalem on a donkey through a sea of palms. He was hailed by his believers as the son of God, the Christ, the Saviour and the King of Kings.

Barabbas had entered Jerusalem in the shadow of night. Now a wealthy man through his tidal wave of crime, he bought his friends, and they would harbour him within the underbelly of the city. Now king of murderers and thieves, he set himself up in a drinking den of iniquity, bedding with the owner, the widow Judith.

Judith's tavern was in the lower area of the city. It was in a labyrinth of streets and alleyways and a perfect place for Barabbas to hide out.

The widow Judith was a strong, hardened woman with a voluptuous figure, but she always seemed to pick men from the wrong side of the tracks. And Barabbas was certainly from the wrong side of the tracks.

He was south of Heaven, east of Eden
and west of Babylon.

Judith was in love with Barabbas. She knew he would never love her back but did not care. She knew how to keep him happy and that made her happy. Besides, she received plenty of love from her beautiful daughter Lydia.

Lydia was the opposite of her mother. She was pure, innocent and naive. She was sixteen, with perfect blue eyes, long golden hair, a slim body and milky white skin.

Lydia was her mother's little angel and would help her run the tavern.

Marcus and Cassis finally arrived back in Jerusalem, exhausted after their adventure. They had failed in their quest to capture Barabbas, but they would never give up the hunt.

THE LAST SUPPER

Marcus knew there was no loyalty among the rats that plagued the city, so thirty pieces of silver were put up as a reward for information as to the whereabouts of Barabbas. Marcus sharpened the spear's head, sensing it was now just a matter of time.

The time had come for the last supper of Christ. Jesus shared bread and wine with his disciples and then, in the still of night, he awaited his fate in the garden of Gethsemane. The disciple Judas had betrayed him for thirty pieces of silver. A Judas kiss revealed Jesus to the soldiers, and without resistance, Jesus was arrested.

Barabbas gorged every supper as if it were his last. Slumped in the tavern, drunk on wine, he kept staring at Lydia, Judith's sixteen-year-old daughter. Judith could see the lust in his eyes. She knew if he wanted something, right or wrong, he would just take it. For her daughter's sake, she slipped out the back door.

Marcus handed Judith thirty pieces of silver. They seemed unimportant to her, but she took them all the same and ran back to her tavern.

Marcus and Cassius gathered ten more soldiers, and into the night and into the bear pit they went.

Judith went to Barabbas, kissed him and whispered sorry. The Romans burst in, blades and eyes flashing. Fights and screams broke out and a volcanic chaos erupted. As Barabbas tried to flee, Marcus hurled the spear, pinning the flesh and bone of Barabbas's arm to the wooden door. The carnage ceased.

Barabbas drew his sword and tried to fight Marcus, but a one-armed Barabbas was no match for one of Rome's finest warriors. Barabbas flung down his sword and declared,

"I am Barabbas; your spear holds me now but not forever. I will be back and sweet vengeance will be mine."

"You won't be back. I will see you crucified and damned to hell," replied Marcus.

"And I have vowed to see you draw your last breath," added Cassius.

At last, the proud Romans had captured Barabbas.

THE CRUCIFIXION

Judgement day arrived, as did a great crowd. Pontius Pilate, the Commander over Jerusalem, had the power to set one prisoner free. He decided to let the people choose. A mob mentality exploded within the crowd. Eventually, the shouts for Barabbas overpowered the cries for Jesus. Against his better judgement, Pilate passed sentence and Barabbas was set free.

For Jesus, it was the sentence of crucifixion.

Marcus was devastated that a good man like Jesus had not been set free. Cassius was devastated as to why an evil man like Barabbas had been set free. Either way, it was out of their hands, and what would be, would be.

Marcus and Cassius were ordered to oversee the crucifixion. Jesus, crowned with thorns, had to bear his own cross, dragging it through the streets, being mocked and mourned along the way. The passion of Christ meant nothing to Barabbas; he celebrated his freedom by getting drunk with the city's low life.

The cross was erected and Christ nailed upon it. As the spikes impaled the hands of Jesus, Barabbas felt the same pain, his hands dropping his wine cup and bottle. He felt sick and went outside to be alone. As the sky turned black, so did his vision. As Jesus passed away, Barabbas passed out.

When Jesus forgave them as they did not know what they had done, Marcus knew he was the saviour and the son of God. He planted the spear in the ground and dropped to his knees. Jesus was dead, but to make certain, Cassius took the spear and pierced the flesh of Christ. Enraged by the actions of Cassius, Marcus knocked him to the ground with a swift blow. He took the spear and snapped it across his knee. He looked up at the crucifixion and declared,

"No more! No more!"

He flung down the broken spear and walked away.

That night, he also walked away from the Roman army, leaving violence for good. Cassius also walked away. Disillusioned with Jerusalem, he was dispatched back to Rome. It was the city he loved as he was still a proud Roman soldier.

VENGEANCE

Barabbas began to have nightmares. He had visions of himself nailed to a cross alongside Jesus. When word of the resurrection of Christ spread, Barabbas became paranoid and decided to leave Jerusalem.

Before he left, he wanted his sweet revenge. He climbed through a window and into the bedroom of a sleeping Judith. He climbed on top of her, putting his hand over her mouth. As she opened her eyes, he spat in them and whispered,

"You traitorous bitch."

He then calmly slit her throat from ear to ear. Suddenly, he heard a noise from the next room. He rushed in and found Lydia waking up. He punched her hard in the face before she could scream out. Barabbas held onto her long golden hair as he raped her, and he laughed as she cried. Once finished, he sheathed his cock and became a shadow in the night.

Barabbas had made the mistake of not killing Lydia. The broken-jawed Lydia went for help, and the word of what Barabbas had done soon spread. His sweet vengeance would now bring on his own downfall.

As he tried to escape from the city, he was captured and beaten by his so-called friends. Even these barbaric dogs believed Barabbas had gone too far. This time, he had crossed a line that disgusted even the worst of the worst.

Pontius Pilate felt he had the blood of Christ on his hands, so he washed his hands of Barabbas, sending him to Rome as a slave and gladiator.

ROME

Barabbas was a natural-born killer, and being a gladiator gave him the power to kill. He killed all that stood before him, and in Rome's arena, he became the people's champion. Barabbas loved the fame, the glory and the lust for blood.

Cassius was appalled by Barabbas's fame and glory. He gained an audience with Caesar and begged Caesar to let him fight Barabbas. He would kill Barabbas in the arena for the glory of the Roman Empire. Caesar was unimpressed until Cassius presented him with a gift; it was the top half of the broken spear, the point still stained with the blood of Christ. Caesar's eyes suddenly lit up. He knew the legend of the spear and believed it possessed great powers. Caesar grasped the spear and Cassius' wish was granted.

Cassius could not sleep the night before the fight. He lay awake remembering the adventurous times he had spent with his old friend Marcus. The places they had been, the people they had met and the sights they had seen. He had not seen Marcus since the crucifixion of Jesus. He wondered where he had gone, where he was now, what he was doing and whether he was even still alive. The one thing he did know was how deeply he missed him and how he wished Marcus was with him now, to support and guide him.

Cassius's thoughts then turned towards Barabbas. He remembered all the crimes he had committed, all the robbings, the beatings, the rapes and the killings. He hated him and detested how, in Rome, Barabbas had become a hero of the arena.

Cassius knew he would have to summon up all this hatred and use it to give him strength for the fight ahead.

The night before the fight, Barabbas woke up, as he did most nights, in a cold sweat. For with the darkness of sleep, nightmares would come. Even with the passing of time, the recurring visions of himself nailed to a cross next to Jesus would still haunt him. For Barabbas was only happy on the sands of the arena, for it was there that he was idolised and adored. Over the years, he had butchered many strange animals and scores of men without remorse, to the cheers of the crowd. He now looked forward to his fight with Cassius; he lay awake, thinking of different ways of bringing down death upon him.

The sun was at its highest point when Cassius and Barabbas entered the arena. The packed crowd welcomed them with a deafening roar. The two men drew their swords and saluted Caesar, the nobles and then the public. The crowd roared even louder and began to chant.

"Barabbas! Barabbas! Barabbas!"

"Barabbas! Barabbas! Barabbas!"

The two men faced each other with their hearts pounding like drums. Cassius had never seen battle before, let alone killed, but he had been trained to fight by one of Rome's greatest soldiers, Marcus Vittori. Cassius was fearless as he believed he had justice on his side. Barabbas feared no man or living soul, and not even death itself.

There was no war of words between them as their swords would do the talking. Cassius took a deep breath and raised his sword and shield.

The time had come and battle commenced.

GLADIATORS

The dual in the sun had begun
Man against man one against one
Both warriors first and last
Their time is now forget the past
They face each other toe to toe
Reigning down blow upon blow
Swords slash and shields clash
Bones shattered and blood splattered
They soaked up the pain like a sponge
Slash after slash, lunge after lunge
For this was no page in a story
This was a fight for death or glory
For this was no surrender or die
This was a mouthful of blood, spat in the eye

The dual in the sun was nearly done
Man against man, one against one
Attack attack a smack and a crack
A cut to the neck, a stab in the back
A kick in the teeth, a kick in the head
Wounds open up and the sand turns red
A voice cries out, "Kill! Kill! Kill!"
The crowd ignites: "Kill! Kill! Kill!"
Eye to eye they barely stand
Face to face still sword in hand
Far too brave to show any fear
But the sun is setting and the end is near
For this was no surrender or die
This was a mouthful of blood, spat in the eye

The fight was over and only one man stood.

Cassius stood over Barabbas with his sword at his throat, ready for the final thrust. The crowd was baying for the kill. Amongst the yelling of the crowd, Cassius could hear only one voice; a voice pleading,

"No more! No more!"

Amongst the hundreds of faces, Cassius saw only one; it was the face of his old friend Marcus. Cassius smiled, dropped his sword and left the arena.

Caesar, embarrassed by the spectacle before him, ordered Cassius to be thrown out of the army and banished from Rome. And Barabbas, only just barely alive, was to be crucified outside the city walls of Rome.

THE VISION

Cassius left Rome with Marcus, their friendship and loyalty unbroken. As they left the city walls, they passed the dying, crucified Barabbas. They stopped and glanced up for a brief moment, and in that moment, they finally saw Barabbas draw his last breath.

Barabbas closed his eyes, and as he fell into the darkness of death, his nightmares now became real, with a vision of Christ nailed to a cross beside him.

Jesus said to him, "I am the son of God. I am the key to the Kingdom of Heaven. My disciples will spread the gospel and sow the seeds of goodness. These seeds will grow and spread across the earth and the words of God shall be heard for thousands of years to come. You are the son of Satan. You are the gate to hell. Through your seeds of rape, your bloodline will soil the earth and evil will spread for thousands of years to come. Now go join your master in hell."

Barabbas was dead.

THE DESTINY

Jesus had worked miracles; he had even raised his friend Lazarus from the dead. Barabbas would have killed a man just to see the light fade from his eyes. Jesus had walked in the light and upon water; he had fed the five thousand and turned water into wine. Barabbas had walked in the shadow of death; he had walked all over those before him. He had fed off the people and got drunk on the wine. Their parallel lives of miracles and murders had ended with them both nailed to a cross.

The eternal battle of good against evil
would continue for all time.

After witnessing the crucifixion of Jesus, Marcus had left Jerusalem to become a preacher of Christ. Now reunited with Cassius, he once again took him under his wing. The two friends left Rome and Barabbas behind them for good. They set out on a new journey with new horizons and adventures ahead of them. Marcus no longer had the spear to guide them, just the words of Jesus and the power of God.

As they began their journey, they looked up at the beautiful blue cloudless sky. They noticed a magnificent eagle floating on the breeze, occasionally flapping its wings.

EPILOGUE

The spear brought Caesar great power for a time, but in the hands of evil men it would eventually bring destruction. The last Roman Emperor to hold the spear was Nero. As Rome burned, Nero fiddled, using the broken spear to make a hellish scream that was music only to Nero's ears.

Maybe the spear burnt in the ashes of Rome, but legends and myths of the spear would appear throughout history. It would bring great leaders and tyrants immense power but, in the end, their downfall. Men like Constantine, Charlemagne, Otto the Great, Genghis Khan and Napoleon.

The last tyrant and madman to hold the spear was Adolf Hitler. Hitler wanted to build an empire, just as the Romans had done before him, but as he gained more power, he also gained insanity. The madness brought him to his knees and to his death. A Russian soldier found the spear, by now just the diamond-shaped tip. It was on a silver chain around the neck of a dead German officer, Hitler. The Russian could see little value in this strange medallion and he sold it on to a US Marine.

After the war, the marine returned home to America, and that's where the legend ends.

The marine was a sergeant named James Vittori.

THE END

The
Diary
of
Angry
Frank

My name's Frank.

People call me Angry Frank

and I've been angry for a long time.

I'm angry with everyone and everything.
In fact, I'm angry with the whole world.

I've been angry ever since my wife died
of cancer and left

me all alone in this two-up two-down
suburban semi.

People say that it's therapeutic to
write things down.

So I've decided to write a diary.

This is the diary of Angry Frank.

DAY 1

Woke up this morning at seven o'clock, same as I do every morning.

I try to get back to sleep but I never can. It's those **blasted seagulls** squawking away, getting in my head and filling it up with anger. God, I hate those ratty, vermin seagulls.

I have breakfast, which consists of a beef and tomato Pot Noodle, a packet of plain crisps, followed by a cup of tea with four rich tea biscuits. In fact, I have the same things for lunch, tea and supper. Well, I don't see the point of having anything else. Besides, it saves on a lot of washing up.

I go to the little shop on the corner after breakfast and buy a few things, including more Pot Noodles, crisps and biscuits.

Before I can get back inside, every morning Gladys, my next-door neighbour, comes out to greet me and we have the same conversation.

"Morning, Frank. How are you today?" To which I always reply,

"Piss off, Gladys."

"Well, you have a nice day."

"Have a nice day – **don't wind me up!**"

I go in and **slam** the door. God, she makes me angry.

I hate her and her cat, too. Her cat, Mr Tibbs, **shits** in the middle of my back garden every day, on my lovely green lawn. God, I **hate** them both.

I don't do much during the day as I'm on benefits. I watch a lot of T.V. but that just makes me angry, especially that Jeremy Kyle. He makes my blood boil. **god, I'm so angry.**

By the time I go to bed, my head is banging with anger and the **voices** inside my head.

I can't **sleeeeeeeep!**

DAY 2

Exactly the same as yesterday.

Ditto.

Ditto.

Bloody ditto.

Angry.

Angry.

Bloody angry.

Blasted seagulls!!!!!!!!!!!!!!!!!!!!!!!!!!!!!!

DAY 3

Ditto.   Ditto.   Ditto.

Seagulls.

Pot Noodle.

Crisps.

Biscuits.

Gladys.

Mr Tibbs.

Jeremy Kyle.

Angry.

Angry. Angry.

Heeeeeeeeeeeeeelp!

DAY 4

Ditto.   Ditto.   Ditto.

Seagulls.

Pot Noodle.

Crisps.

Angry.

Piss off Gladys.

Slam door.

Mr Tibbs.

Angry.

Biscuits.

Jeremy Kyle.

Pot Noodle. Pot Noodle. Pot Noodle.

Going mad.
Arrrrrrrrrrrrrrrrrrrrrrrgh!

Day 5

Day five was different.

I woke up as usual, with the seagulls demonic decibels squawking in my brain.

I could take it no more.

I remembered I had an old air rifle and a box of pellets up in the attic. I went up to the attic, dusted down the gun, loaded it and rushed to my upstairs back window.

I opened the window and aimed the gun.

Bang! Bang! Bang!

Squawks and feathers everywhere. Looked like one bird down and two wounded.

I still had it, I thought proudly. I quickly closed the window and went downstairs for breakfast.

As I had breakfast, I smiled for the first time in years. I was happy.

I was still smiling as I walked round to the little shop. What's this – chicken and mushroom Pot Noodle? I'll try them and these, cheese and onion crisps. What about these, custard creams, why not?

As usual, before I could get to my front door,

"Morning, Frank. How are you today?"

"Piss off, Gladys."

"Well, you have a nice day."

"Have a nice day – don't wind me up!" and slam went my door.

I was having a lovely lunch. My taste buds were going crazy, and as for the custard creams, pure heaven. The enjoyment of my banquet was soon destroyed though, for out of the corner of my eye and through my kitchen window, I saw Mr Tibbs.

There he was, Mr Tibbs, Gladys's black cat, roaming round my garden like he owned it. There he went right in the middle of my lawn, a stinking shit. Right, that's it. I rushed upstairs, got my gun and took aim.

Bang!

Got him.

Right in the shoulder.

That'll teach him.

He limped his way behind my shed and hid himself away.

Today Was a Good Day.

DAY 6

I woke up this morning later than normal. There were no wretched seagulls squawking down by the bins. This was pure bliss. What a happy start to the day, and it got better, for while I was in the little shop on the corner, I treated myself.

Chow mien Pot Noodle, beef crisps and bourbon biscuits.

"Morning, Frank. How are you today?"

"Piss off, Gladys!"

"Well, you have a nice day."

"Have a nice day – don't wind me up!"

"Oh, Frank, have you seen Mr Tibbs? Just that he didn't come home last night and I'm a bit worried as I thought I heard gunshots the other day."

"No, I haven't."

Then slam! goes my front door.

Lunchtime comes, and as I'm sitting down enjoying my gourmet meal, who do I see?

It's only **Gladys!** Poking her nose over my fence. Must be looking for her **damn** cat.

That's good, she's gone. Hang on a minute, she's back. 82 years old and she's standing on some stepladder peering over my fence. Right, that does it. I rush upstairs and get my gun.

Bang!

Right in the neck and she falls to the ground.

All I can see is one of her slipper-wearing legs.

Bang!

Right in the ankle. That should put a stop to her. I return to my lunch with a big grin. **Lovely.**

After supper, I sat down to a bit of David Attenborough on the TV with a cup of tea and some bourbon biscuits. I had closed my eyes and Attenborough had taken me to some kind of savannah nirvana.

All of a sudden, my tranquil state was broken by the sound of **blaring sirens**

I looked out through my front curtains and there was Gladys on a stretcher, getting put in the back of an **ambulance.**

Suddenly, there's **banging** on my door, and I'm boiling with rage.

"What do you want? I'm trying to watch Attenborough."

"Sorry, sir, your neighbour's been shot by what appears to be an air rifle. We were wondering whether you had seen or heard anything. Also, she's very concerned about her cat. She thinks it might be in your back garden. If possible, we would like to take a look, please."

"No, I haven't seen or heard anything.

Now piss off, copper."

"If you don't cooperate, sir, we'll be back tomorrow with a warrant to search the premises."

"I said piss off, copper!"

DAY 7

I woke up early, skipped breakfast and rushed to the little shop on the corner. I bought loads of Pot Noodles, crisps and biscuits and rushed straight back home. Once inside, I took my shopping, a kettle, a mug, a big plastic drum of water, toilet paper, a bucket, a radio and my gun upstairs then up into the attic.

The attic was dusty but snug. There was an old mattress, blankets, a light and power for the kettle and radio. If I needed the toilet, I'd just go in the bucket. Then I'd pour it out of the VELUX window and it would slide down the roof tiles and into the gutter, sorted.

Breakfast, lunch, tea and supper soon passed. The radio was not the same as the T.V. but it sufficed.

I enjoyed all the new flavours I was experiencing, especially the crisps – Worcester sauce. Wow.

I slept with a crescent moon and the stars above me. The night sky was my new ceiling, glowing through the VELUX.

The lazy coppers never turned up, either.

Perfect!

DAY 8

Morning came and so did the **coppers,** banging on the door.

I stayed quiet and just watched all the action from the VELUX window. There was a lot of shouting and **banging** on doors. They had got through to the back garden and started nosing around.

"**Here, Sarge!** Over here behind the shed."

Damn, they've found Mr Tibbs. Damn, he's still **alive!**

More banging on doors and shouting.

"Right, break the door down. I want a full search and an arrest. Go! Go! Go!"

"Yes, Sarge!" "Yes, Sarge!"

"All clear, Sarge!" "No one here, Sarge!"

Stupid coppers.

Can't even search a house properly. Time for a cup of tea and some biscuits.

Being stuck up in the attic gave me a lot of time to think and contemplate exactly what I had done.

Was I angry, was I happy, or was I just **sad?**

After all, seagulls were just birds trying to find food for themselves. Gladys was just a sweet old lady who was a good neighbour and good friend of my late wife. Even Mr Tibbs wasn't that bad a cat. Well, maybe he was, but he didn't deserve to be shot.

My wife would be ashamed of the man I had become, and I was **ashamed** of myself.

DAY 9

I woke up to the sound of the police sergeant **barking** out orders again.

"**Right, you lot!** I want another search of the property from top to bottom. He's gotta be hiding somewhere."

"Yes, Sarge!" "Yes, Sarge!"

I could hear them poking around the rooms, knocking things over, probably making a right old **mess.** Suddenly, the sergeant annoyingly noticed the loft hatch.

"What about up there? Has anyone been up in the loft and searched the attic?"

"No, Sarge!" "No, Sarge!"

Right, that's it. No **bastard** copper's going to take me alive.
I put the rifle barrel under my chin.

"Goodbye, cruel world."

Bang!

DAY ??????

I'm now in **prison.** Got a three-month sentence and I deserved it.

The pellet I fired never killed me. It just left a **nasty** scar under my chin.

Gladys and Mr Tibbs made full recoveries too, which was a relief. In fact, Gladys stuck up for me in court. She remembered me when I was a **nice** man and a **good** neighbour.

She had also promised my dying wife that she would look out for me, **God** bless her.

I quite enjoy prison life. The food is fantastic, especially breakfast. I either have **porridge** or a **bacon** sandwich. Both delicious and much better than Pot Noodles.

There's table tennis and pool. OK, I have to play on my **own** but I don't mind.

Plus, **a miracle** has occurred.

I'm actually **happy** for the first time in years.

I've got a cellmate called Dave. He's my best friend. OK, he might give me a slap now and again, but he's still my best friend. In fact, he's the only friend I have.

Every morning, I make Dave a cup of tea and we have the same conversation.

"Morning, Dave. How are you today?" To which he always replies,

"Piss off, Frank!"

The End

(No old ladies, cats or seagulls were killed or injured in the writing of this story.)

Poems

The Captain

I am the captain of the ship until the day that I die
or until the ocean waves goodbye.
Like a unicorn in a uniform
I surf the tide and ride the storm.

With Poseidon beside me and the night skies to guide me
I seek the hands of faraway lands.
Across the seven seas and where the four winds blow
I dance to the tune of the ebb and the flow.

The places I have been, the treasures I have seen
the strangers I have met, in a life without regret.
I have seen skies of red, orange, fire and gold.
I have seen oceans of green, turquoise, black and blue.

Sometimes mermaids sing sweet songs in my head
sometimes I hear the screams of the unburied dead.
Warm days spent under the glory of the sun
cold nights spent alone and chilled to the bone.

Now the eye of the hurricane, it may see me coming
it can wink and it can blink but it can never take my heart.
For I am the captain of the ship and my heart will go down with it.

And when the devil's breath blows me deep into the abyss
and I choke on the spit of his saltwater kiss,
I will not cry when it's my time to die and the ocean waves goodbye.

I will dance with mermaids, down on the seabed
and sing and laugh with the unburied dead.
Forever the captain, in the heart his ship.

The rise and fall of the bare-knuckle fighter

Now Murray was a mauler and a backstreet brawler
When he raised his hands he grew bigger and he grew taller.
He climbed every mountain as he rose up from the gutter
He chewed up opponents like a chainsaw in butter.

He fought for the money but glory was the prize
And you never saw fear in his stone-cold eyes.
Under the moonlight or down in a basement
In a car park or out on the pavement.

It was violent, it was brutal and some would say sick
A five-knuckle punch, a butt and a kick.
Now Murray's hands were fast when he was in his prime
But not as fast as the hands of time.

His body was bruised, it was used and abused
It was ripped and torn and badly tattooed.
And as he got older, his eyes grew colder
The beatings got harder, his kids needed a father.

So now he drives a lorry to take home the pay
But he still reminisces about back in the day
When Murray was a mauler and a backstreet brawler.
He can still raise his hands; he just looks a little smaller.